THE COSMIC VENDING MACHINE OF THE GALACTIC LAUGHINGSTOCK

A Novel

Philip Mazza

Also by Philip Mazza

From Under a Tree
Book One; The Harrow Saga

Shadow in the Flame
Book Two; The Harrow Saga

Children at the Gate
Book Three; The Harrow Saga

The Child of Fire
Book Four; The Harrow Saga
(Coming 2025)

The Neon Hive

The Quantum Gardener

At the End of it All

Beneath the Ashen Sky

I Know God is a Cat

The Road to Stillwater

THE COSMIC VENDING MACHINE OF THE GALACTIC LAUGHINGSTOCK

A Novel

Philip Mazza

OMNI PUBLISHERS

www.philipmazza.com

Omni Publishers of New York
ISBN 979-8-9924526-2-4
Printed in the United States of America

First Printing: April 2025

For anyone who's ever felt like an alien observing the human race. You are not alone.

AUTHOR'S INTRODUCTION

Alright, alright, you beautiful, bewildered sacks of protoplasm, gather 'round. You're likely squinting at this . . . artifact, this agglomeration of tree corpses and ink stains, wondering who's responsible for this particular strain of mental mange. That would be me. Consider me your friendly neighborhood peddler of paradoxes, your sherpa through the intellectual quicksand. My moniker? Let's just say it's a series of noises strung together with the vague intent of identification. And don't expect a recitation of prestigious awards, because those are usually obtained through bribery, blackmail, or sheer dumb luck. I'm simply a fellow traveler who's swallowed a bit too much cosmic dust and decided to cough it all back up on you. Sorry about that.

The whole messy conception of this book? It started predictably enough, with a cruise, no less. Yes, I'm aware, that's practically a confession of bourgeois guilt right there. My physician, a well-meaning but catastrophically inept quack, insisted on a "recharge," a "reset," a chance to "unplug from the matrix," or whatever new-age claptrap he'd been peddling at the time. The poor fellow didn't grasp that my matrix is permanently fried, emitting sparks and questionable smells at all hours of the day. But who am I to argue with a nice, young man holding a prescription pad? Hawaii, French Polynesia, the whole nine yards of sun-drenched cliché. Palm trees swaying like drunken hula dancers, suspiciously fluorescent cocktails garnished with miniature umbrellas, and sunburns in places where the sun frankly has no business being.

Now, cruises, as I'm sure many of you have experienced, are essentially floating circuses of human folly. There are the all-you-can-eat buffets, where otherwise rational adults transform into ravenous locusts, devouring miniature corn dogs with the ferocity of a starving badger. There are the choreographed dance numbers, performed with the robotic precision of wind-up toys powered by pure desperation. And then, of course, there's the relentless cacophony of announcements, reminding you of all the overpriced trinkets you could be acquiring, the dubious spa treatments you could be indulging in, and the thrilling bingo games you could be losing money on. It's a relentless assault on the senses, designed to distract you from the chilling realization that you're adrift on a massive steel coffin, hurtling toward an inevitable date with the seabed.

So, picture this: there I was, attempting to choke down a Mai Tai that tasted suspiciously of industrial cleaner, watching a throng of tourists attempt to hula with all the grace of a herd of startled elephants, when the revelation struck me. What if aliens were observing this spectacle? What if they were on a similar voyage, except instead of admiring tropical sunsets, they were taking guided tours of Earth, meticulously cataloging our unique brand of self-inflicted lunacy? What if they were chuckling at our political skirmishes, gasping at our consumerist fervor, shaking their multiple heads at our collective inability to navigate a revolving door without causing a pile-up?

The notion, like a particularly persistent earworm, latched itself onto my cerebral cortex and refused to let go. I began scrawling notes on soggy cocktail napkins, doodling grotesque alien faces on the backs of travel brochures, much to the bewilderment of my fellow passengers, who probably assumed I was undergoing some sort of slow-motion mental implosion. One woman even offered me a stress ball shaped like a dolphin. I declined, politely. I prefer my stress raw, unadulterated, and shaped like impending doom.

And that, my friends, is the convoluted and slightly unhinged origin story of this book. It's a lighthearted, satirical, and hopefully slightly unnerving peek at humanity through the multifaceted eyes of extraterrestrial visitors. Envision it as a cosmic field trip, a chance to detach yourself from the chaos and observe our collective buffoonery from a secure, slightly inebriated vantage point. I've filled the narrative with characters who are just as baffled and bemused by our shenanigans as I am. There's Zog, the jaded multi-limbed bartender, who's seen more galactic idiocy than you've had lukewarm beers. There's the fastidious Trixlian family, struggling to comprehend why Earthlings seem to favor reality television over actual reality. And then there's the young, naive Vrilp, whose only ambition is to purchase a set of "Alternative Facts Dice," because let's face it, who among us wouldn't secretly yearn for a set of dice that always land in our favor? I know I would, if I could find them at a reasonable price. Perhaps I will invent them, that way I am guaranteed to make all the money, which I will promptly lose on another ill-advised cruise to help this doctor get money for his vacation. He has already been planning to travel to Las Vegas.

Now, some of you may be anticipating a profound, earth-shattering message lurking within these pages, some groundbreaking insight into the human condition. But I'm not in the business of delivering tidy resolutions or comforting platitudes. My aim is to provoke the awkward questions, the ones that make you fidget uneasily and perhaps spill a little coffee on your metaphorical lap. Is humanity destined for oblivion? Most likely. Are we beyond the possibility of salvation? Who can say, really? But are we endlessly amusing to observe in our descent into the abyss? Absolutely.

So, crack open this book, pour yourself a drink—maybe something strong enough to make you forget your social security number—and prepare to laugh, cry, or stare blankly into the void like a cow watching a passing train. Whatever you do, just make sure you feel something.

Because the worst thing a person can do when faced with absurdity is to sit there like a sack of potatoes and say, "Well, that's just how it is."

And as our intergalactic rubberneckers are about to find out, Earthlings have never been famous for apathy. No, no—shortsightedness, arrogance, and an uncanny ability to elect the worst possible people, sure. But not apathy. Although now that I think about it, if someone packaged stupidity into a collectible dice set, it'd probably outsell everything else. Might even come with a rulebook nobody reads.

CHAPTER 1: ARRIVAL AT EARTH

It was a wonderous galactic day in the year 2025 when the interstellar star cruiser GLOMP-77 drifted into Earth's orbit, its chrome hull shimmering like a promise no one had actually made. Suspended above the planet's fragile atmosphere, it reflected the light of the distant sun with the smug confidence of a species that had long since abandoned the need for uncertainty. Below, Earth just kept spinning, dumb as a brick, and the folks down there hadn't a clue they were about to be the main attraction in a cosmic peepshow, observed by aliens like they were a bunch of particularly stubborn zoo animals who refused to mate on cue.

Inside the cruiser, the passengers felt a gentle, almost apologetic vibration as the ship's cloaking systems activated. This was to be expected. Cloaking technology, after all, was not some mysterious force but rather a piece of machinery, and all machinery, no matter how advanced, harbored a deep and abiding resentment toward the creatures who built it.

Most of the passengers were already shuffling toward their excursion tenders—small vessels designed to transport tourists to planets too primitive to build proper spaceports. They were giddy to witness the bewildering spectacle of human existence, to watch the strange little creatures scurry about their lives with all the conviction of beings who thought their opinions mattered.

But then a youngster named Vrilp—who had not yet suffered the indignities of employment, debt, or existential despair—came to an abrupt and violent halt. His gelatinous eyes widened in amazement.

Before him stood a vending machine, flashing in garish, blinking letters:

THE COSMIC VENDING MACHINE OF THE GALACTIC LAUGHINGSTOCK.

The machine hummed with quiet, capitalist menace. It was the intergalactic equivalent of a roadside gift shop that sold both commemorative snow globes and beef jerky of dubious origin. Behind its glass, an array of useless yet strangely compelling trinkets rotated slowly on motorized shelves, each representing a planet deemed too ridiculous to be taken seriously by the rest of the civilized galaxy.

There was "Molly the Mining Mule Action Figure" from Gritrock-7—a toy that celebrated backbreaking labor as the pinnacle of technological achievement. There was the "Flat Universe Model Kit" from Flattopia—a do-it-yourself project that steadfastly ignored all known laws of physics, astronomy, and common sense. And, of course, there was the Zorgon-9 Protein Bar, which proudly declared "Now With 4% Actual Protein!"—a selling point so depressingly low that it could only mean previous versions contained none at all.

But Vrilp's attention latched onto something truly special:

"Alternative Facts Dice" from Earth.

A set of six-sided dice where every roll displayed the number the roller wanted it to be. Not the number dictated by physics or logic or the oppressive tyranny of mathematical probability—but the number that felt right in one's mind, the number that served a purpose.

The packaging, in bold, triumphant letters, screamed:

WHERE EVERY ROLL IS A WINNER, AND TRUTH IS WHATEVER YOU NEED IT TO BE!

It continued, because of course it did:

Never lose a game again! These revolutionary six-sided dice always display the number you desire. Perfect for gamblers, politicians, and individuals with an aversion to reality. A must-have for aspiring demagogues, casual liars, and Earth leaders who shall remain nameless but possess a deep affection for golden towers and headwear in colors that resemble an enraged citrus fruit.

At the bottom, a tiny warning label had been affixed, likely to appease some humorless regulatory body:

Caution: May cause cognitive dissonance in rational beings. Prolonged use may lead to detachment from objective reality. Side effects include misplaced confidence, public office, and possible collapse of democratic institutions.

Vrilp reached for his credits, his entire small, pulsating body quivering with anticipation.

"I need this," he whispered.

"Absolutely not," said his mother, Tralg, without looking up from her excursion pamphlet, which promised thrilling visits to "The Land of Free Speech Zones" and "A Nation Governed by the Electoral College, Which is Neither a College Nor Particularly Electoral."

"But— but— " Vrilp wailed. "I could always win!"

"That's precisely the problem," Tralg snapped. "No child of mine is growing up to be a politician. We're here to observe primitive cultures, not to become them. And we don't buy souvenirs from designated Galactic Laughingstocks," Tralg reminded him. "It sends the wrong message."

And with that, she gently but firmly guided her sulking offspring toward the tenders, leaving the Alternative Facts Dice to spin in their glass case, waiting for the next eager buyer who preferred a world where numbers, like facts, were merely suggestions.

Vrilp crossed his appendages, huffing in frustration like any child denied their cosmic aspirations. "This is so unfair. The last time we visited Blorptar-9, you let me get the collapsible sun lamp!"

"That was educational," Tralg said. "This is just . . . depressing."

Vrilp sulked all the way onto the tender, dragging his feet—or at least the closest biological equivalent—while shooting wistful glances at the vending machine. The Earth dice gleamed enticingly under its fluorescent spotlight, mocking him with their unattainable allure. Meanwhile, just outside the cruiser, the real Earth continued its oblivious spin—unaware it had been reduced to a novelty item for intergalactic amusement.

Before boarding the tenders, each tourist affixed a delicate, bracelet-like device to their wrist. The gadgets, known as Invisibells, emitted a faint, reassuring pulse that bent light and sound around their bodies, rendering them invisible to any unwitting Earthlings. A marvel of Eldorin engineering, the Invisibells ensured that even the nosiest human wouldn't notice an alien peering over their shoulder—at least in theory. But some passengers quickly realized that moving too fast caused an odd, watery shimmer, as if reality itself were mildly inconvenienced by their presence.

The ship's automated AI, EXCURSIA, crackled to life, its synthetic enthusiasm dialed up to a level that could make even a black hole feel self-conscious. "Welcome, GLOMP-77 passengers! Welcome to Earth! A charming little dust mote in a vast, unfeeling universe! Your trip has been generously sponsored by Spacely's Space Tours, and we hope you have a delightful time observing the primitive natives!"

The passengers funneled into the boarding tenders with the grim determination of beings who had spent their entire lives following instructions, even when they weren't particularly good ones. Each step, each buckle of a safety harness, each polite nod to a fellow traveler reeked of a species-wide resignation: this is what we do now.

Once the tenders were filled, secured, and sealed up tighter than a politician's tax records, they detached from the GLOMP-77 with the grace of high-society meteorites, gliding toward Earth with the utmost decorum. The crafts, having learned from the embarrassing failures of earlier models, automatically adjusted their shielding to avoid the spontaneous combustion problem—a design flaw responsible for a number of unplanned cremations on planets with less accommodating atmospheres. There was still an unfortunate whiff of roasted tourist on the official record, but Spacely's Space Tours had done a wonderful job pretending otherwise.

As the tenders descended toward their designated landing sites, hushed oohs and ahhs rippled through the cabins. Perhaps it was the strange, uncoordinated sprawl of human civilization that had them in awe. Or maybe it was the velvet-lined seating, which had been engineered to mimic the embrace of a rich but emotionally distant grandmother. Or maybe—just maybe—it was the crisp, floral-scented air circulation system, designed to prevent anyone from asking uncomfortable questions like "What does space actually smell like?"

Whatever the case, the passengers clutched their Invisibell bracelets, adjusted their posture, and prepared for what they had all come to see: a species still convinced it was in charge of something.

A Trixlian family, consisting of Gorvax, Mleeb, and their two children, Spliv and Grib, were particularly thrilled.

Trixlians, for those unfamiliar with them, resembled giant iguanas—scaled, long-tailed creatures, each one meticulously neat, with a penchant for order and a slightly unsettling desire to catalog everything. Their bodies, though slow-moving, were surprisingly nimble when it came to crossing t's and dotting i's. As such, they had become avid travelers, and Earth was one of the most popular stops on the Galactic Misunderstandings Tour.

"We have arrived!" Gorvax announced, clapping his scaled hands together, which echoed loudly in the silence of the cabin. "I hear Earthlings call their most prosperous nation 'America.' It's the political center of everything!"

"Doesn't sound very appealing," Mleeb muttered, inspecting her nails. "We could've gone to Alpha Centauri, you know. They have spas."

Spliv, who had just turned eight, yawned. "I heard Earth people argue a lot," he said, turning to his younger sister. "I think they argue more than they talk."

"Are we sure they can't see us?" Grib asked, her large yellow eyes squinting suspiciously at the windows, where city lights glimmered far below them. "We're invisible, right?"

"Of course, dear," Mleeb reassured her, though there was an edge to her voice that suggested even she had some doubts. "The tourists are invisible. The humans have no idea we're even here. It's all part of the experience."

"But . . ." Spliv began, tapping his bracelet with a clawed finger. "What if one of them looks right at us? Will they see us?"

Before Mleeb could respond, the tour guide, a humanoid alien from Braxalon-7 named Glorpnax-17, stepped forward. His smooth, aquamarine skin shimmered like an overpriced souvenir, and his six fingers clutched a long silver staff, the universal sign of someone who takes themselves way too seriously. He raised a hand to quiet the passengers, who weren't actually making any noise but had the audacity to look like they might.

"Now, my dear guests," Glorpnax said, his voice radiating the warmth of a car salesman who knows he's about to unload a lemon, "I must remind you that even though you are invisible, these humans are—how shall I put this delicately?—paranoid, unpredictable, and alarmingly well-armed. They are not quite the gentle, open-minded creatures you may have read about in those charming intergalactic brochures. They have a tendency to react with hostility to anything they don't understand, which is quite a lot . . . well, almost everything. Do not attempt to interact with them. Keep your bracelets on at all times, and, above all, keep your distance. If you're seen, it will not end well. They are dangerous creatures."

Gorvax scratched his forehead, which was an impressive feat considering he had no forehead. "Dangerous, you say?" he asked, his curiosity ignited. "What is it they do?"

"They shout," Glorpnax explained, his tone as grim as a documentary narrator right before the commercial break. "And worse. They do not welcome outsiders, especially ones who look different from them. Which is pretty much everyone. If your bracelet malfunctions and you find yourself visible, do not make noise, do not make eye contact, and under no circumstances should you attempt to explain anything rationally. That only agitates them further."

Grib's yellow eyes sparkled with uncontainable glee. "Would they throw things at us?" she whispered.

"No, no," Glorpnax sighed, shaking his head. "They may, however, try to sell you something. And trust me, you do not want to buy anything from them. Their goods are, at best, useless trinkets and, at worst, products designed to make you buy even more useless trinkets."

He looked solemnly at the group. "Some of them call this capitalism. Others call it a free market. Either way, it's the most effective trap in the galaxy. Proceed with caution."

Mleeb grabbed Spliv and Grib and gave them a hug. "Remember, children, take good notes on what you see. This will be helpful with your schoolwork."

Spliv quivered with excitement. "You mean we get extra credit for witnessing the collapse of an entire civilization?"

Mleeb patted his head. "Of course, dear. And if it's especially catastrophic, you might even get a certificate."

***

Back on the ship's lower deck, Xarth sat at the bar. The bar was dimly lit with soft, flickering lights that illuminated the array of alien drinks on display. Xarth, an angular, multi-eyed creature with translucent skin that shimmered like starlight, looked out over the slowly spinning Earth. His long, thin limbs rested on the counter, fingers wrapped around a glass that was half full with an intoxicating substance known only to his people.

Xarth wasn't the usual tourist on these excursions. As an Oth'kal, his species had evolved from deep-sea predators who thrived in the weight of gas giants' atmospheres. His body, built for underwater life, now adapted to space travel, allowing him to swim through the void with a fluid grace that his fellow travelers could only envy. Despite his beauty and serenity, there was something unsettling about his presence. The way his eyes, four of them—two in the front and two at the back of his skull— moved independently, scanning everything and nothing at the same time, made him seem more observant than he was letting on.

Xarth swirled the drink, the liquid glowing faintly as he stared into it. His thoughts were distant, whirling like the currents of his home world. He had seen many civilizations rise and fall, but Earth . . . Earth was something else entirely. Something that didn't make sense.

"Another drink?" asked Zog, the bartender, who had long ago accepted that sentient beings would rather be confused and intoxicated than just confused.

Xarth nodded, barely looking up. His hand shook slightly as he reached for the glass. "You know," he muttered, "I remember when they had actual ideas about leadership on this planet. Some of them even believed in science." He took a sip and frowned. "Now they elect people who lie for a living. And those lies . . . people eat them up. Don't even question the taste."

Zog laughed, a strange wheezing sound. "I've been to Earth a few times. I think you might be overestimating them."

Xarth stared into his drink. "I don't know. Maybe they were always this way. Maybe I just couldn't see it." He leaned back, exhausted by the weight of time and the confusion of Earth's cycles. "How did they get so . . . disconnected?"

Zog refilled his drink. "You mean the ones who wear the hats and listen to the loudest voice in the room?"

"Yeah," Xarth sighed. "Those."

CHAPTER 2: THE BAR

Xarth had visited Earth before. In fact, he had visited it so many times he had lost count, which, for a species with a perfect memory and an aversion to exaggeration, was saying something. He slumped at the bar of GLOMP-77's less-than-reputable drinking establishment, a dimly lit space known simply as "The Bar." It was named by the cruise line's original owner, a surly, twelve-eyed being who found creativity exhausting and eventually walked out the airlock in what many described as an elaborate statement on nihilism. Others argued he had simply forgotten to put on his gravity boots, which was a common problem among beings with more eyes than sense. Either way, no one changed the name of the bar. There had been a brief attempt to rename it "The Celestial Lounge," but customers revolted, citing a lack of dignity in ordering a drink from a place that sounded like a waiting area in an intergalactic dentist's office.

Zog, the current bartender, was less dramatic. He had eight arms, seven of which were dedicated to mixing drinks, and an eighth that was exclusively for shaking its fist at customers who asked for complicated cocktails. He slid a glass of something toxic and glowing toward Xarth. "I call it the Cosmic Regret," he said, polishing a glass with one of his many tentacles. "It pairs nicely with existential despair and poor life choices." Zog had once considered using that line in a promotional advertisement but realized that most of his customers already knew what they were getting into.

"You're not going down to the surface?" Zog asked, already knowing the answer but needing conversation to keep himself from pondering his life choices. It was either that or start questioning why a creature with so many appendages had chosen bartending instead of something more practical, like high-stakes organ smuggling.

Xarth peered at his drink, which was starting to glow faintly. "I don't do Earth anymore. Last time, I had a little hope. Thought maybe they'd get their act together. I came back a century later, and they were setting their rivers on fire. Fire, Zog. In water. And they just shrugged and kept doing whatever caused it in the first place."

Zog nodded solemnly. "I saw the footage. That's tough to do. Takes real commitment to stupidity. Gotta respect it."

Xarth took a sip and winced as his drink dissolved part of his tongue. It would grow back. Probably. He had learned not to ask what was in it. The last time he did, Zog had gotten wistful about his homeworld's bioluminescent sludge fields, and Xarth had lost his appetite for a week.

"So, what's the itinerary this time?" he asked, already regretting the question.

Zog pulled up a holographic brochure and read from it in a dramatic voice. "First stop: the so-called political capital, Washington D.C.! See how a nation once built on democratic ideals has turned its governing bodies into a glorified clown rodeo! Gasp at their elections, where the candidates with the most money win! Watch their legislative process, which involves a great deal of yelling, posturing, and ultimately doing nothing! Observe as they debate whether or not basic human survival is a luxury!"

Xarth groaned. "They ought to just replace . . ." He paused, searching the dusty filing cabinets of his brain.

"What the flurp do they call it . . ." More pausing. More dust. "Oh, right. Congress."

He took a long, theatrical sip of his drink. "They should scrap the whole flurping thing and replace it with a giant betting pool and be done with it. Would be more honest. At least when a casino robs you blind, it has the decency to hand you a free drink first."

Zog scrolled further. "Ah, they're also taking a detour to visit something called 'Florida Man.' Apparently, it's a highly localized phenomenon that produces news headlines like 'Florida Man Fights Alligator in Drive-Thru' and 'Florida Man Tries to Trade Baby for Store Credit.'"

Xarth massaged his temples. "Florida Man isn't a single man. It's a lifestyle."

"A way of being," Zog mused. "A cultural identity?"

"A testament to the fact that no matter how many times a species discovers fire, there will always be someone who insists on setting themselves on it to see what happens."

Zog nodded appreciatively. "Deep."

He shrugged, already moving on. "And of course, no tour is complete without a visit to their news networks, where journalists spend hours debating whether or not facts are real."

Xarth exhaled sharply. "Once upon a time, reporters exposed corruption. Now they just argue about what reality is while their corporate overlords sell car insurance."

"And adult diapers," Zog added. "For people so outraged they literally soil themselves. It's a thriving market."

Zog wiped down the bar with a rag that had possibly developed sentience. It whimpered softly. "You know what your problem is, Xarth? You're nostalgic. You think Earth was ever something better."

Xarth frowned. "It was."

Zog snorted. "Oh sure, back when they only had two world wars instead of nearly three. When their science was about discovery and not arguing on the thing they call the 'internet.' When they went to the Moon and then immediately forgot how to go back. Real golden age."

Xarth pointed a clawed finger. "They were trying. They had ambition. Now? They argue over which fast-food mascot is the sexiest."

Zog raised a tentacle. "To be fair, have you seen that one with the red pigtails? She's got a sort of . . . powerful energy."

Xarth groaned and waved him off. "I refuse to have this conversation."

"You've got to admit, though, that's pretty entertaining," Zog said, pouring himself something that audibly wept as it hit the glass.

Xarth sighed and stared at the planet spinning outside the window. "It's like watching a species do everything possible to fail a survival test."

Zog took a sip of his drink. "And yet, somehow, they keep passing."

They watched in silence as the tiny blue-and-green sphere spun below, bustling with life, contradiction, and the peculiar ability to create both symphonies and viral videos of people falling off ladders.

"Alright, maybe I'll tune in for a bit," Xarth muttered, pulling up a feed from the tour group's perspective.

On-screen, an alien child pointed at a group of humans chanting slogans at a political rally. "Mom, what's this about?"

Xarth took a long sip of his drink. "It begins."

Zog grinned. "Told you it'd be fun."

The bar lights flickered as the ship's automated system adjusted for artificial sunset. Somewhere on Earth, a man was probably setting his backyard on fire to prove lizards controlled the government. In another part, a billionaire was considering charging people for air.

And in the middle of it all, humanity carried on— laughing, screaming, building, breaking, and proving, once again, that logic was optional, but spectacle was forever.

CHAPTER 3: THE TOUR BEGINS - OBSERVING AMERICAN POLITICS

As the intergalactic tenders descended from the GLOMP-77 toward Earth's surface, it was clear that the alien tourists had been mentally prepared for their cultural immersion. They weren't sure what they were about to witness, but they had heard enough about Earth's antics on the galactic grapevine to at least know it would be strange. Glorpnax-17, the ever-enthusiastic guide, stood before them with a face gleaming with poorly calibrated optimism.

"You're about to witness the greatness of Earth's political system," Glorpnax said, his tentacles waving like a misguided cheerleader. "Behold, the birthplace of freedom, democracy, and . . . well, confusion. Don't mind the mess. It's part of the charm!"

The tourists, invisible to Earth's oblivious inhabitants thanks to their Invisibells, settled into their assigned spots in the air-conditioned tenders. The tenders, which looked like coffee makers with wings, hummed obediently down to Washington, D.C., the beating heart of America's government, or at least its digestive system.

Upon landing, the alien passengers disembarked, stepping onto the manicured lawns and marble steps with the same quiet reverence one might have when visiting a historically significant train wreck. They observed the leaders of the free world engaged in their primary duties: shaking hands, dodging accountability, and pretending to read important documents. The tourists took notes. Some even wept.

Glorpnax gestured toward the big white building, the one with all the history and none of the wisdom. "We begin here," he said, "the mighty symbol of America's power. Or at least, that's what the brochures used to say. It is called the White House" His grin stretched in a way that suggested he had seen too much of the universe to take any of it seriously.

Inside, the tourists beheld America's leader deep in discussion with another human. The scene was historic, in the sense that everything happening in it would eventually be rewritten to sound more dignified.

Gorvax, a tall, scaly Trixlian who looked like he might have once been a philosopher in another life (or at least had aspirations to be one), raised his clawed hand. "Excuse me, Glorpnax," he asked, his voice oozing confusion. "Why is the leader of this place . . . well, orange?"

Mleeb, Gorvax's mate, added, "And why does he speak in a way that seems to mock reason and logic? Shouldn't the leader be . . . intelligent?"

Glorpnax chuckled, a noise that sounded like a broken toaster. "Oh, that's the beauty of Earth. Their leader rose to power not because of intelligence, but because he was a master of entertainment. He knows how to sell things—especially red hats and vague promises. On this planet, it's an art form, really."

"And who is that next to him?" asked Mleeb. "The pale one with the kind of face that looks like he is still deciding whether to be handsome or just wealthy."

"Oh, that's an advisor," Glorpnax said. "The richest man in the world. His wealth is larger than the wealth of 99% of the nations on Earth."

"What does he do with all that wealth?" Grib asked. "Does he help other humans?"

Glorpnax just laughed. "No. He's the kind of human who carries himself like someone who had just remembered he owned gravity but wasn't sure how to turn it off. You see he's a man who sells electric cars to people who hate public transportation, launches rockets for a species that can't keep its own planet clean, and digs tunnels because he was bored. He once spent forty-four billion dollars on a website where strangers insult each other for free. People call him a genius. He agrees. So did his newfound friend, the one they call 'president.'"

Grib frowned. "So, what is their relationship?"

Glorpnax smiled. "Their relationship is a beautiful mess—a cosmic bromance fueled by mutual admiration, transactional tweets, and an unshakable belief that reality is just a poorly moderated subreddit. The president sees the billionaire as the only man rich enough to make his ideas look reasonable, while the billionaire sees the president as proof that anyone, literally anyone, can be in charge of things."

Spliv, the older of the two Trixlian children, scribbled in his notebook, but his expression was one of perplexed concern. "So, I do not understand. It seems you are saying this president is just . . . a figurehead, then?" he asked.

"No, no," Glorpnax said, shaking his tentacled head. "He's the leader! In his mind, at least. His followers believe him to be a genius. If you squint hard enough and ignore a few things—like basic logic—it almost makes sense!"

Then this so-called leader and his wealthy companion disappeared into another chamber, where a herd of humans immediately began shouting at them. The leader, in turn, made even louder shouts back. The shouts did not seem to communicate information so much as assert dominance, like two rival swamp creatures croaking at each other in the dark.

Grib, the slightly older Trixlian with a curiosity that matched his skepticism, tilted her head. "But if he's a leader, why do the people keep yelling at each other? Shouldn't they agree with him?"

"Well, yes," Glorpnax said, "but humans, you see, enjoy shouting more than agreeing. It's how they communicate their disagreements. The louder they shout, the more they believe they've won."

"Like a contest?" Grib asked.

"Exactly. Only no one knows what the prize is." Glorpnax gestured. "This is the very heart of this nation's leadership. Historically, this place was full of grand ideas and lofty goals. These days, it's just a place where decisions are made based on whatever gets the most attention. You'll see."

The Trixlian family looked around in awe, still unsure of what they were looking at. It was all a bit too much to digest in one go. But they had only begun.

Meanwhile, as the shouting continued, the human leader—whose hairstyle could only be described as "mimicking a wig-wearing cat in the throes of a bad day"— was indeed the star of the show.

Glorpnax walked the tourists through the basics of American politics. "Now, watch closely," he said, eyes wide with overcompensated excitement. "This is the most entertaining aspect of Earth. You'll learn how their leaders are chosen. The human concept of democracy, or rather the idea of democracy, is quite fascinating. It's like a game show where the contestants have no idea that they're in the game."

Spliv frowned. "Wait—so they pick their leader by voting for him?"

"Not quite," Glorpnax explained. "They vote for who makes the best promises, and then they scream at each other until someone has to leave the room. The real winner is whoever can keep the most people entertained." He paused. "And that's usually the one who can yell the loudest without saying anything of value."

"But what about their laws?" Gorvax asked, still struggling to wrap his head around the absurdity of it all.

"Ah, laws and courts," Glorpnax replied with a grin, "a self-correcting mechanism of their system. "Well-designed you may think, until the leader deprives the courts of their power or packs them with loyalists." Glorpnax shook his head in disgust. "The laws, as interpreted by the courts, stretch and twist to match whatever sounds good that week. The whole thing turns into a game show. And guess what? You don't even have to be smart to be the host."

"Right. That's why they have news programs to explain everything," Grib said, squinting at her notes like there might be an answer in there somewhere.

"Exactly! You've got it!" Glorpnax congratulated, clearly impressed. "But that's another self-correcting mechanism easily distorted by the leader, as needed. The leader learns how to control and censor information, rewrite history books to make him look brilliant, hire people to make sure nobody says the wrong things, and slap a big patriotic bow on top. But most importantly, the leader does whatever it takes to keep the audience consuming their drivel."

"Drivel?" Grib repeated, antennas twitching.

"Drivel," Glorpnax said, savoring the word like a fine delicacy. "It's the stuff you feed people when you want them to feel smart but stay stupid. Its words arranged in a shape that resembles meaning, but if you poke it too hard, it collapses like a cake made of wet sand. And the best part?

The more they consume, the hungrier they get. Beautiful system, really."

"But what about truth?" Grib asked.

"Truth?" Glorpnax chuckled, patting Grib on the shoulder like a parent humoring a child who still believed in bedtime stories. "Truth is whatever keeps the machine running smoothly. If an inconvenient fact jams up the gears, you sand it down, paint over it, and call it an upgrade. The real trick is making people believe they've discovered the truth themselves—makes them defend it like a favorite chair, even if it's on fire."

Grib flipped back through her notes, eyes wide. "So, what about freedom?"

Glorpnax burst out laughing. "Oh, Grib. You really are new how things work here. Freedom is the best product ever invented. People will buy it, fight for it, even die for it, without ever asking what's actually in the box. You see, real freedom . . . actual, unfiltered, do-whatever-you-want freedom . . . is terrifying. Chaos! Madness! Neighbors stealing your food, gravity working only on Tuesdays. So instead, they get a nice, prepackaged version: just enough choices to feel in control, just enough rules to keep things tidy. And the best part? If they ever feel trapped, they can blame themselves for not using their freedom correctly. Genius, really."

Grib stared at her notes, then at Glorpnax, then back at his notes. Her face drooped in sadness. She had started this conversation hoping for clarity, maybe even a sense of order in the universe. Instead, she felt like a malfunctioning circuit, sparks flying, logic shorting out. Freedom wasn't real, truth was adjustable, and drivel was the fuel that kept everything running? It was all so neatly packaged, so perfectly absurd, that it had to make sense—but it didn't. Not to her. Not to her poor, overworked brain. She shut down her notepad with a sigh, wondering if ignorance really was bliss, and if so, where the hell she could get some.

As the group wandered through the various rooms of the White House, the Trixlians kept making notes, trying to decipher how a country of over 300 million people could possibly function under such a system. The whole thing felt like a cosmic joke, and unfortunately, the punchline hadn't landed yet.

After a few hours of wandering, the tourists were whisked away to the next stop: the U.S. Congress. It was no better. In fact, it might have been worse.

The moment they entered the chambers of Congress, they were greeted with the sight of a group of humans yelling at each other over something that, in the grand scheme of things, didn't matter. One side was arguing over whether a bill should be passed in three minutes or five, while the other side was too busy shouting that the other side didn't deserve to make a decision in the first place. The whole situation looked like a kindergarten class where everyone had been given a microphone and no one knew how to turn them off.

Glorpnax, not missing a beat, clapped his tentacles together. "Ah yes, here we have the pinnacle of American democracy! Two sides, each trying to get their own way, each convinced they are right, and both believing that the louder they shout, the smarter they seem."

Mleeb, who had been unusually quiet, leaned over to Gorvax and muttered, "On Trixlia, we don't argue for the sake of it. We debate until we reach a logical conclusion."

Glorpnax overheard. "Yes, well, here on Earth, it's a little different. They argue for the sake of appearing right, not for reaching a conclusion."

"And what do they do with the decisions they make?" Gorvax asked, genuinely curious.

"They go back to their television studios and social media sites, and announce it with great fanfare," Glorpnax answered. "And then nothing changes."

"Nothing?" Spliv asked, looking horrified. "So, all of this shouting and arguing means . . . nothing?"

Glorpnax chuckled. "Exactly. It's a show, my young friend. But as long as they can sell ads during the breaks and get views on social media, it's considered a success."

***

Back at the bar on GLOMP-77, Xarth leaned back in his stool, watching Earth drift closer. His glass, which had started as a refreshing cocktail of neon-blue mystery liquid, was now a sad puddle at the bottom. It seemed as though the universe had given up on offering any new thrills for the jaded traveler.

Zog, the tentacled bartender of questionable hygiene, scuttled over and nudged Xarth with one of his more generously sized appendages. "So, what do you think? Earth politics getting better?" Zog's tone suggested a kind of detached amusement, like he was watching a toddler attempt to solve a Rubik's cube while strapped into a rocket chair.

Xarth took a long, almost painfully slow sip of his drink, then tilted his head back, as though trying to get a better look at the Earth through his increasingly bleary eyes. "Better? They used to have a functioning system," Xarth muttered, lowering his glass. "They used to think history was something you could learn from. You know—those crazy ideas about rhymes and patterns and lessons. Now?" He spread his arms, as if to encompass all of humanity's blunders in one sweeping gesture. "Now, it's just a collection of shouting matches in overpriced suits. They don't even see the pattern anymore. Hell, they don't even know history has a pattern."

Zog tilted his head, which was a remarkable feat considering the sheer number of appendages involved. "Pattern? You mean like... a pattern of what, exactly?"

Xarth shook his head, like a teacher correcting a very slow pupil. "I mean that history rhymes, Zog. It's like a song with a melody you should've memorized by now. You know—the rise and fall of tyrants. They always sound so sweet at first, don't they? They're like sweet talkers at the bar, promising you the world, and boom—before you know it, you're living under a regime that makes no sense whatsoever. It's the same damn tune every time."

Zog's tentacles shuffled with mild irritation. "I see," he said, clearly not seeing at all. "So, you're saying they're repeating mistakes?"

Xarth gave a rueful chuckle, almost amused by the simplicity of the question. "Not repeating. Recycling," he said, now becoming more animated as the alcohol fueled his sense of cosmic injustice. "This is why they are a lesser species. They have short memories. They don't learn from the past. They recycle it. It's a new season of The Tyrants We Love to Hate show. And humans? They don't get it.

Not a damn one of them. You could put Hitler or Stalin in a new suit with a new haircut and they'd follow him to the ends of the Earth if he promised them some piece of new technology and some 'alternative facts.'"

"Wooo . . . Hitler . . . Stalin . . . yeah, I've heard of those guys," Zog said, polishing a glass with an appendage or two. "Real go-getters."

"Yeah, it's a hell of a show. And they love it. They love it like they love their reality TV and social media feeds."

Zog blinked—if a creature with three dozen eyes could blink—then let out a sound that might have been a sigh or an attempt at a cough. "Okay, okay, history rhymes, tyrants rise, fine. I get it. But what's your point here? You think they're doomed or something?"

Xarth's lips curled into a grim smile. "Doomed? No. They're just... distracted. They can't even tell the difference between an evil dictator and a new flavor of potato chips." He slapped the bar with one of his large, clawed hands, as if to punctuate his point. "It's the news networks and social media, you see. We're talking about the same old game of controlling information, manipulating the story. The trick's the same—sell 'em a narrative, and they'll swallow anything. Hell, they'll even beg for seconds."

Zog, attempting to be philosophical, paused in his perpetual cleaning of the counter. "So, all those shouting matches? They're just distractions?"

Xarth nodded slowly, savoring the weight of the truth. "Yep. It's all for show. They think the shouting matters. But really, all they're doing is positioning themselves for the next big commercial break, the next feed. As long as they can keep the people angry, they can keep the wheels of the tyranny machine greased. It doesn't matter if it's a dictator or a demagogue, it's the same engine, running on the same fuel—fear and outrage. And those networks? And those social media sites? They make it all possible."

"Hell of a show," Zog muttered.

"In a sense," Xarth said. "The trick is every human leader knows something the rest of them don't."

"Oh yeah? What's that?"

"That branding works just as well on people as it does on soda. You take a corrupt billionaire, slap the right slogan on him, and suddenly he's the savior of the working class. Take a walking disaster, who's dumb-as-all-hell, and put him in a fancy suit, and presto—genius. A guy who barely survived boot camp? Instant war hero. Or a guy who avoided military service due to bone spurs? Puff—tough guy. And don't get me started on the gurus. One minute they're exploiting their followers, the next they're glowing with divine wisdom. People don't fall in love with leaders. They fall in love with the ad campaign."

"Damn. They're idiots," Zog said.

"In so many fascinating ways," Xarth agreed.

Zog's tentacles twitched, like he was trying to fan a bad smell out of the air. "But they'll figure it out eventually, right? No way this keeps working."

Xarth snorted, a bitter sound that only partially escaped his throat. "Figure it out? They've been running this con since the first ape convinced the others he could make it rain by dancing. It's not about figuring it out. It's about wanting to believe. These humans, they're not just buying snake oil. They're lining up to drink the stuff, begging for refills. And the real kicker? Deep down, they know it's all horseshit. But admitting that means admitting they've been had. So, they double down, triple down, quadruple down until they're so far down they can't see daylight anymore. It's a cosmic joke, really. The punchline? They keep electing the very bastards who are picking their pockets and setting their house on fire. And they call it freedom."

Xarth chuckled, a noise like a washing machine choking on a bag of nails. "And the leaders, they're so deep into their own spin that they'll never get out. They just keep riding the wave, hoping the next big scandal is enough to keep the population of lemmings distracted from the fact that they're turning into puppets on strings. That's the real magic trick, Zog. The puppet masters never get called out. They're behind the curtain, pulling the strings, writing the ad campaigns, while everyone else fights over the marionette's next move."

"Lemmings?" Zog asked.

"Tiny rodents. Run off cliffs because the guy in front does. Nature's way of proving peer pressure kills." Xarth waved a hand.

Zog, by now fully immersed in this weirdly cynical monologue, nodded sagely, although it was clear he was still processing. "So... you're saying that it's all just one big distraction?"

Xarth finished his drink with one last gulp, feeling the remnants of his cynicism fizzle out like an old bottle of soda. "Exactly. Their history books are full of leaders who promised to 'fix the system,' and when they didn't, someone else came along and pretended they could do better. But the story? The real story is always the same. It's not about fixing anything. It's about keeping people watching while the same corrupt systems just shuffle around in a circle, looking for the next sucker."

Zog tapped his tentacle thoughtfully against the bar. "So... they never get out of the loop?"

Xarth leaned in, eyes narrowing in a way that suggested he wasn't entirely sure of the answer himself. "Maybe some of them do, Zog. Maybe some of them catch a glimpse of the loop and start to break free. But those are the ones who end up... more confused than before."

Zog's eyes—if you could call them that—narrowed, just a little. "You think they'll catch on someday? Humans, I mean."

Xarth considered this for a moment, swirling his empty glass, watching it catch the last bit of dim light. "They'll catch on when they're too tired to care anymore. When they've shouted themselves hoarse and burned themselves out. Maybe then, they'll look up and realize they've been played all along."

Zog snorted, wiping the counter once again. "Well, they've got plenty of time, right? I mean, Earth's been around for... well, forever."

Xarth smiled wryly, tapping his empty glass for a refill. "That's the problem. They've had forever... and still haven't figured it out."

Zog brought over a new bottle. Xarth stared at it.

"Made in China," he chuckled bitterly. "Like everything else." But it wasn't of course.

Zog poured the liquid into a glass.

Xarth swirled the liquid. "Oh, and did you hear about their president? Bought some kind of electric chariot from his billionaire pal." He shuddered. "Still using cars. Pathetic. They haven't even cracked cell-transporter technology yet."

Zog chuckled, a sound like air leaking from a punctured lung. "Ah, yes. The combustion engine. A charmingly inefficient method of converting dead dinosaurs into noise pollution. And the electric ones? Just moving the pollution to a different location, really. They're still stuck in these metal boxes. I think they like being stuck. Part of their quaint charm, I guess"

"Charm?" Xarth's eyes widened, two in the front, two in the back, giving him a perpetually surprised expression. "My good friend, they willingly sit in traffic for hours, breathing exhaust fumes, listening to insipid audio programs, just to get to a job they hate so they can buy things they don't need. That's not charm, that's . . . elaborate self-torture."

Zog shrugged, a feat that involved his many appendages moving in a strangely unsettling, synchronized motion. "Maybe they enjoy the misery. You know, a species thing. Like how some species enjoy flinging themselves off cliffs. Like those lemmings things." He poured himself a shot of something green and bubbling. "Besides, what's the alternative? Walking? They're evolved to walk. But they gave that up a long time ago."

Xarth took another sip of his drink, wincing slightly. "I suppose you have a point. It's just . . . disheartening. They have the potential, Zog. They invented string theory, composed symphonies that could make a nebula weep, and yet they're still clinging to these . . . antiquated modes of transportation." He paused. "And they actually pay for the privilege! To sit in their tiny boxes, slowly killing themselves. It's . . . beautiful really, in a terrible, self-destructive sort of way."

"That's Earth for you," Zog grinned, or at least it looked like one. "A cosmic train wreck you can't look away from." He paused, then added thoughtfully, "Speaking of transport, have you seen Glorpnax's hover-scooter? Apparently, it runs on sheer desperation. It's quite a sight to behold."

Xarth shuddered again. "Sounds like Glorpnax is de-evolving into a human."

Zog chuckled or it could've been a gurgle of phlegm unable to make its way down one of his many throats.

"You know," Xarth continued, "I prefer to observe the self-destruction of humanity from a safe distance. Preferably with a high-proof beverage and a healthy dose of cynicism. Those humans on Earth are going to continue to do what humans are going to do. And their continued idiocy is something that I think everyone should watch." He swirled his glass and tilted it back taking a last sip. "Another, my friend."

And so, as Earth was but a speck in the vast universe, the two sat in silence—one pondering the endless absurdity of human history, the other pondering whether or not he'd overcharged for the last round of drinks.

CHAPTER 4: THE COSMIC CONFUSION OVER DEMOCRACY

The tourists continued to watch the goings-on at the United States Capitol, which had once symbolized the highest ideals of a fledgling nation. Now, it primarily functioned as an elaborate set piece for television shouting matches. It was a building full of people elected by other people who often regretted it immediately.

The guide, Glorpnax-17, a highly advanced alien with historical accuracy and deep, existential disappointment, hovered before the group of intergalactic tourists.

"Remember," Glorpnax announced, "this was once the beating, sputtering, wheezing heart of American democracy. Once the pinnacle of self-governance. Now it's an exceptionally tedious live-action soap opera."

Gorvax, the Trixlian patriarch, tugged on his a Invisibells bracelet to ensure he was still invisible to the humans then adjusted his spectral viewing visor and observed the chaos inside the chamber. Several humans in ill-fitting suits were gesturing wildly at one another. One was holding a sign that said, "Think of the children!" Another held one that said, "No, think of our children!" A third held one that simply read, "I DO NOT CONSENT," though it was unclear to what.

"Fascinating," Gorvax muttered. "On Trixlia, leaders are chosen based on competence and intelligence. Doesn't seem to the be case here, at all."

The tourists moved closer to the observation deck, where a heated debate was taking place on the floor of Congress. A representative from Texas was shouting about something called 'woke sandwiches.' A senator from Vermont was demanding the dismantling of the 'billionaire yacht industrial complex.' A representative from Florida was reading Bible verses that did not pertain to anything in particular.

Spliv, the young Trixlian, blinked his large, reptilian eyes. "Are they trying to solve problems?"

"Absolutely not," Glorpnax said. "They are performing. The humans of this region have realized that genuine problem-solving requires effort, compromise, and expertise. Unfortunately, none of those things are telegenic."

Grib was taking notes in his universal learning tablet. "So, their primary function as leaders is to make the other leaders look foolish?"

"Correct," Glorpnax said. "This is known as 'owning the opposition.' It is their highest form of political discourse."

"Fascinating," Gorvax said again, his frills shifting in confusion. "If no problems are being solved, how do they maintain power?"

"They engage in a highly sophisticated system of pretending," Glorpnax explained. "For example, observe that man there—"

The tourists all turned their attention toward a particularly rotund senator, who was passionately denouncing government spending while simultaneously funneling millions of public dollars into a project called The National Research Center for the Scientific Study of Beard Lengths in American History—which, coincidentally, was based in his home state.

"You see," Glorpnax continued, "humans have mastered the ability to say one thing while doing another. It is considered an advanced survival skill in this culture."

The Trixlian children scribbled frantically. "And the people accept this?"

"Of course," Glorpnax said. "Because they believe the other side is much worse. This is called 'lesser evilism' and is a crucial component of their electoral process."

Mleeb, the Trixlian mother, narrowed her eyes. "But if everyone is simply choosing the lesser of two evils, doesn't that mean they are still constantly choosing evil?"

"Yes," Glorpnax said. "That is why they are so tired all the time."

At that moment, a vote was called. Bells rang. A flurry of activity overtook the chamber. Legislators rushed to the front of the room, eager to cast their ballots on an important piece of legislation called the Let's All Pretend to Fix This Act of 2025. No one had read it. No one knew what it contained. This was not considered a problem.

A tour group of human schoolchildren walked by, led by an exhausted history teacher who had clearly given up on inspiring them.

"And this is where democracy happens," the teacher said, rubbing his temples. "Or at least, this is where it's supposed to happen. Let's keep moving before I say something that gets me fired."

Spliv pointed at the human children. "What happens to them?"

Glorpnax sighed. "They are taught that they can grow up to change the system. Then they grow up and realize they cannot."

"Oh," Spliv said. "That sounds sad."

"That's because it is," Glorpnax said.

***

Far from the noise of Congress, far from the important people pretending to do important things, Xarth sat at the GLOMP-77's dimly lit bar, contemplating the bottom of his glass. It was a very old, very deep glass. If he stared long enough, he figured he might fall in and never have to climb out.

"I remember when they still passed laws," he muttered, more to his drink than to anyone else.

Zog wiped down the counter with one of his many appendages, mostly for show. Hygiene standards in deep space were lax at best. "They still pass laws."

"No," Xarth said. "They pass things called laws. But now they're either symbolic nonsense that accomplishes nothing or five-thousand-page monstrosities that no one reads, stuffed with loopholes, favors, and other things no one voted for."

Zog slid him another drink. "So, what changed?"

Xarth swirled the liquid in his glass, watching it catch the neon light like a firefly trapped in bureaucracy. "They figured out you can make more money selling outrage than fixing problems."

Zog grunted. It was a sound he had practiced after realizing humans found it wise and reassuring. "That bad, huh?"

Xarth chuckled. "You ever notice they're always running for something? Re-election. Higher office. Another fifteen seconds of attention here and there on their social networks. These people don't govern. They campaign. It's the only thing they actually know how to do."

Zog poured himself a drink—an unusual act, considering he had no mouth, no digestive system, and no biological need for alcohol. He mostly did it for effect. "And the people?" he asked. "They just let it happen?"

Xarth exhaled. "They've got bills to pay, kids to feed, bosses to keep happy, algorithms to appease. They've got a million things to stress about before they even get to democracy. And by the time they do, they're too exhausted to do anything but pick a color—red or blue—and hope it all works out. And if it doesn't, well, they'll blame each other, because that's easier than blaming the game."

Zog exhaled sharply through what looked like gills. "Sounds like a scam."

Xarth laughed. "Of course it's a scam. But here's the beauty of it—" He tapped the side of his glass for emphasis.

"They have to believe it's not. They have to think they're in control, or the whole thing collapses."

Zog thought about that for a long time. Or at least for about five seconds, which, in the world of intergalactic bartending, was considered deep contemplation.

Then he said, "Want another drink?"

Xarth nodded.

Outside, Earth spun on, the grand illusion still intact.

CHAPTER 5: MEDIA - THE GREAT DISTRACTOR

The next stop on the tour was a news station. It was a perfect cube, a great, gray box squatting in the middle of a paved wasteland, as if it had crash-landed there and decided to stay. It had no windows. Windows implied a need for outside perspective, and outside perspectives led to dangerous things like thinking. Instead, every side of the cube was covered in giant screens, each broadcasting a different flavor of hysteria. On one, a red-faced man screamed about tax rates. On another, a woman in a tight blazer gestured at a chart that proved, once and for all, that everyone who disagreed with her was an idiot. The third screen featured a panel of experts nodding solemnly while discussing whether hurricanes were real or just government-funded performance art.

A cluster of excited tourists hovered just above the pavement, invisible to the locals but humming with curiosity like overcaffeinated bees. Spliv and Grib, the two young Trixlians, furiously scribbled notes into their data slates, trying to make sense of a species that did not appear to make sense. Their father, Gorvax, wore the carefully constructed expression of an adult who had long ago accepted nonsense as the dominant human trait. Their mother, Mleeb, flicked her tongue in distress. It tasted like asphalt, burning wires, and anxiety. The taste of human civilization.

"This place smells like fear," Grib observed.

"Yes," said their tour guide, Glorpnax, adjusting his shimmering translator device. "That is an intentional part of the business model. Fear smells like engagement. Engagement smells like revenue. Revenue smells like victory."

Glorpnax waved his arm, and the walls of the station flickered, then vanished. One-way invisibility—perfect for tourists who wanted the thrill of witnessing a culture collapse without actually getting their hands dirty.

Inside, the newsroom buzzed like an electrified ant farm. Reporters typed furiously, editors gestured like deranged conductors, and giant screens flashed breaking news:

DEADLY STORM HEADING FOR FLORIDA!

SOME SAY THE STORM IS FAKE!

IS WEATHER A LIBERAL HOAX?

Spliv squinted at the screens. "They don't know if the storm is real?"

"Oh, they know," Glorpnax assured him. "They just haven't decided which version of reality is most profitable."

At the center of the chaos, two men sat behind a sleek news desk, their expensive suits tailored to look expensive. One was rodent-thin, nostrils twitching as he jabbed a finger at the screen behind him. The other was bull-shaped, his tie strangling his thick neck. A voice from nowhere introduced them:

"Welcome to Dueling Realities! Tonight's topic: Hurricane Calvin – Storm of the Century, or Just More Fear-Mongering?"

The screen behind them played footage of people drowning.

"This is a manufactured crisis," said the rodent-man. "The so-called 'hurricane' is nothing more than a strong breeze being exaggerated by the weather-industrial complex!"

The bull-man's face turned the color of spoiled meat. "That's insane. People are dying."

"Oh please," the rodent sneered. "They say people die all the time, yet I've never seen it personally."

"That's because you work in a studio and never leave the building."

"Exactly! So how can we be sure death even exists?"

Glorpnax turned to his tourists. "Observe: Both men have access to the same information, yet each presents a different version of reality. The goal is not truth. The goal is to make you angry enough to keep watching."

Spliv's face twisted in horror. "But—but—facts exist!"

Glorpnax patted the boy on the head like he was a doomed pet. "Not here."

Grib narrowed her eyes. "If facts are just opinions, how do they function as a species?"

"Poorly," said Glorpnax. "Very poorly."

Inside the studio, the debate took an unexpected turn.

The rodent-man scowled at the footage of destruction. "The hurricane conveniently fits the radical environmentalist agenda. If the storm is so real, why have I never personally been in a hurricane?"

The bull-man sputtered. "You live in Arizona! There are no hurricanes in the desert!"

Rodent-man's eyes glowed with triumph. "Exactly! So how do we know they even exist?"

The broadcast cut to commercials.

First, a diet pill promising to melt fat while possibly melting organs. Then, a medication for a disease invented last week. Finally, an app that made you look younger in exchange for your biometric data and soul.

When the debate resumed, something was different.

The rodent-man now claimed the hurricane was real, a biblical reckoning. The bull-man insisted it was a hoax, a scam, an illusion.

Spliv's mouth fell open. "They changed sides?"

"They do that sometimes," Glorpnax said. "It keeps the audience engaged."

"But why argue at all?" Mleeb asked. "If the hurricane is real, wouldn't it be more helpful to tell people to evacuate?"

Glorpnax sighed the sigh of a being who had explained something obvious a thousand times and expected to explain it a thousand more.

"Helpful, yes," he said. "Profitable, no. You see, my dear Mleeb, humans do not worship truth. They worship the illusion of choice. If you tell them a hurricane is coming and they must evacuate, they resent you for treating them like children. But if you give them two conflicting narratives—one that says 'Run for your lives!' and another that says 'Nothing to worry about, keep shopping!'—then they feel powerful. They get to decide if they believe in the hurricane.

"And once a person decides something, they'll do anything to defend it. They'll scream at their neighbors, disown their relatives, and, most importantly, keep watching to make sure they were right. Ratings skyrocket.

Advertisers throw money at the network. The CEO buys another yacht, which he will name Ethics just for the irony.

"Meanwhile, the hurricane doesn't care. It will drown both the believers and the skeptics with perfect indifference. And the next day, the survivors will argue over whether the floodwaters were a government conspiracy."

Glorpnax adjusted his shimmering translator device and smiled. "That, my dear Mleeb, is how a free press sustains a free market. And how both of them ensure the population remains just intelligent enough to operate a cash register, but not intelligent enough to question why they're doing it during a hurricane."

In a glass-walled lounge high above the studio, the network's CEO sipped an overpriced cocktail and grinned at his trembling assistants.

"They're eating it up," he said. "Ratings are through the roof."

"But sir," one assistant whispered, "what if the storm is actually dangerous?"

The CEO chuckled. "Then they'll keep watching to see if they survive."

***

Far above the planet, inside the GLOMP-77's lounge, Xarth swirled the neon liquid in his glass and listened to the muted hum of the intergalactic jazz band. Zog wiped a speck of spilled liquor from the counter with one of his many tentacles.

"You're brooding," Zog observed.

"I'm always brooding," Xarth muttered.

Zog nodded. "Fair."

Xarth stared at his drink. "Used to be, journalists uncovered the truth."

Zog snorted. "Sounds exhausting."

"It was," Xarth admitted. "But at least it meant something." He took a slow sip. "Now, they don't uncover the truth. They curate it. They shape it for an audience. Left, right, doesn't matter—just keep them mad and make them watch the commercials."

Zog refilled his glass. "So, what's the big difference?"

"The difference," Xarth said, tapping the counter, "is that people used to be lied to against their will. Now, they actively subscribe to the version of reality they like best."

Zog considered this. "Seems efficient."

Xarth laughed bitterly. "That's the problem. It works too well."

He glanced at the screen behind the bar, where a news anchor was reporting live from a flooded town.

The anchor held a microphone in one hand and gestured toward a ruined neighborhood. "We're standing in what some are calling the worst storm of the decade—"

The feed cut abruptly to an in-studio commentator.

"We can't verify that claim," he said smoothly. "After all, who's to say what 'worst' really means? And can we trust these so-called 'weather experts'? Are hurricanes just nature's opinion?"

The screen flashed to a commercial for bottled water.

Zog sighed. "Same old Earth, huh?"

Xarth swirled his drink, watching the storm on the screen. "Nah," he muttered. "Used to be, people just argued about the news. Now they don't believe it exists."

The storm raged on, whether they believed in it or not.

CHAPTER 6: A VISIT TO THE HEARTLAND - LEARNING WHAT A 'CULT' IS

It was a bright and sunny day in the land of the free, which, as it turned out, was neither especially free nor particularly land-like anymore, as most of it had been bought by corporations that turned topsoil into parking lots.

Glorpnax, ever the chipper tour guide, shepherded his invisible tourists through a throbbing mass of terrestrial devotion. The crowd was a sea of red, not the noble kind that spoke of sacrifice, but the cheap polyester kind that screamed bulk discount. Their shirts proudly declared 'Merica!, as if the first syllable had been a waste of time. On stage, their leader, the president — a man with a face like an undercooked potato and hair that defied physics — waved his hands, and the crowd moved as one, like a school of particularly gullible fish.

"Notice how the president's followers react," Glorpnax said, his voice buzzing through the tourists' earpieces. "They treat him not as a flawed being, but as an infallible deity."

The tourists nodded, their various appendages twitching with curiosity.

Spliv observed the rally with wide, iridescent eyes. "So, this is what humans call a cult?" he asked.

Glorpnax cleared his throat. "Technically, yes, but in this culture, they call it a 'movement.'"

At that moment, the president on stage threw his arms in the air and the crowd erupted in a chant so synchronized it could have been conducted by a hive-mind.

"BUILD THE THING! BUILD THE THING!"

Spliv tugged at his father's sleeve. "What thing?"

"I'm not sure," Gorvax admitted, tapping his translator device. "It appears to be some kind of abstract concept. Possibly metaphorical, possibly a very large wall, possibly a pyramid scheme."

The president grinned, revealing a set of teeth that had either been aggressively whitened or completely replaced with polished ceramic. He waved both hands, and the crowd roared as though he had just provided the secret to immortality.

"What exactly has he done to earn this level of adoration?" Mleeb, the mother, asked.

Glorpnax flipped through his briefing. "It appears he has convinced them he is one of them, despite overwhelming evidence to the contrary."

Spliv squinted at the projection. "So, he's poor?"

Glorpnax chuckled. "No, quite the opposite. He lives in a golden tower."

Grib frowned. "Then how is he one of them?"

"Well," Glorpnax explained patiently, "he has mastered the art of speaking like a very dumb but very confident uncle at a family gathering. Observe."

The president leaned into the microphone. "Listen. Listen. I know things. I know the best things. The smartest things. The so-called experts? They don't want you to know what I know. But I know it. Believe me."

The crowd howled in approval, some throwing their hats in the air, which were immediately sold back to them at a higher price.

Spliv frowned. "But he didn't actually say anything."

"Exactly," Glorpnax said. "A brilliant strategy. By saying nothing, he ensures that everyone hears exactly what they want to hear."

Mleeb tilted her head. "And they don't notice?"

"No," Glorpnax said. "In fact, they get angry if you point it out."

A man in the crowd began foaming at the mouth as he screamed something about "fake news." His wife patted him reassuringly while their child, no older than six, held a sign reading, 'Make Earth Flat Again.'

Grib leaned in. "What happens when he does something completely contradictory to what he just promised?"

"Ah!" Glorpnax's eyes lit up. "That's the beauty of the system. You see, when that happens, his followers will declare that he's 'playing four-dimensional chess' and that mere mortals cannot comprehend his strategy."

Spliv rubbed his head in thought. "So, it's an advanced form of denial?"

"Exactly."

A woman in the front row threw herself toward the stage, clutching at the president's podium with the fervor of a medieval peasant grasping a holy relic. "We love you!" she shrieked.

The president smirked and adjusted his tie. "I love you too."

The woman collapsed, overcome with joy. Paramedics rushed in, though it was unclear if they were there to assist or to sell rally merchandise.

"Fascinating," Gorvax murmured. "On Trixlia, we don't have any of this nonsense."

"Yes," Glorpnax said, sighing. "That is why you're here, I suppose. To learn. To make sure you never do."

Just then, a female journalist attempted to ask the president a question. The president narrowed his eyes. "You, are very unfair. Very dishonest. Very nasty. Everybody hates you."

The crowd turned, and the journalist, sensing the sudden shift in energy, backed away quickly.

Grib observed the reaction with concern. "So, anyone who disagrees with him is declared an enemy?"

"Correct," Glorpnax confirmed. "It keeps things simple."

"Doesn't that make it dangerous?" Spliv asked.

Glorpnax shrugged. "Not for him."

On cue, the president's motorcade pulled up, an absurdly large collection of black SUVs with tinted windows that made it look like a funeral procession for democracy. The president gave the crowd one last thumbs-up and with his small hands started to pump his fists.

"He's doing the fist thing again," Glorpnax observed. "We've seen this over and over again."

"The . . . fist thing?" asked one of the alien tourists.

"Yes," Glorpnax explained. "It's a curious Earth custom. When delivering pronouncements of questionable veracity, their leader is fond of clenching his hand and thrusting it skyward. It's been done for centuries and is meant to convey strength, conviction, and a complete disregard for historical context. I call it—The Tiny Fist of Tyranny. It's a classic."

The human president's right arm shot upward, outstretched, with his palm down. It was a gesture that seemed both aggressive and vaguely comical. "Does it show the world he's strong," Grib asked.

Glorpnax winced. "The technique varies, of course," he continued. "Sometimes it's a slow, deliberate pump, designed to emphasize each syllable. Other times, it's a rapid, frantic jab, meant to whip the crowd into a frenzy."

The tourists gasped, enthralled. On of them blurted "Is that how they show affection?"

"It's . . . unsettling," another said. "It's like a child throwing a tantrum."

"He seems terribly proud of that hand," Vrilp whispered to his mother. "Does it have special powers?"

Tralg sighed. "I doubt it," she replied. "I think it's merely a symbol. A way to tell the masses that he's in charge."

Glorpnax chimed in, "You are correct. Earthlings are easily swayed by symbols."

Another tourist piped up, "So is that which makes them feel in charge? Is that a sign of true greatness?"

"Why do they tolerate it?" another asked. "Why don't they simply laugh him off the stage?"

Glorpnax chuckled. "Because Earthlings are simple creatures. Some of them genuinely believe in him. Others are too apathetic to care. And a significant percentage are just there for the spectacle."

"These Earthlings," Tralg added, "they're a bit stupid aren't they. And you can't exactly help them now, can you? Some planets just specialize in breeding the lesser intelligent. But hey, that's what makes it so much fun to watch."

Glorpnax shook his head. "It's a tragic cycle, for sure," he said. "They empower the very individuals who seek to exploit them. And then they wonder why their society is falling apart."

As the president's small hands continued their relentless pumping, those in black clothing assigned to protect him from other humans, whisked him away to what was either a government meeting or a golf course.

The aliens prepared to depart. The crowd, meanwhile, kept chanting. A single, unified, obedient noise, like a chorus of well-trained robots. The tourists stepped through the invisible barrier of their observation field, shaking their heads.

Grib whispered. "So, this is how democracy ends?"

Glorpnax checked his notes. "Oh no, it's not over. It just changes shape now and then. Like a gelatinous lifeform. The key is keeping the people distracted long enough so they don't notice who's really in charge."

The tourists climbed aboard their transport tender and ascended to their next destination, their understanding of Earth's political system both expanded and thoroughly baffled.

***

Meanwhile, back in the ship's bar, Xarth swirled his drink and sighed, the universal sign of a sentient being resigning itself to the absurdity of existence. The drink, a concoction of liquefied minerals from a dying star, was technically illegal in twelve star systems due to its unfortunate side effect of making drinkers ponder their insignificance in the grand cosmic order. Xarth had been drinking it for years.

Zog wiped down the counter with one of his many tentacles, an unnecessary motion since the bar had long ago been coated in an anti-microbial gel that repelled all known contaminants. But he liked the ritual. Gave him something to do while people like Xarth wallowed in existential dread.

"You look like a man who's watched history repeat itself one too many times," Zog said.

Xarth nodded. "I've seen a lot of planets go down this path," he said. "Starts with a little paranoia, a little fearmongering, and before you know it, half the population is convinced their neighbors are conspiring against them while the other half is stockpiling canned goods for an apocalypse that will never come."

Zog slid him another drink, because this was clearly going to be one of those nights.

"So, this leader of theirs, the one they call 'president,'" Zog said. "You know, the orange one. He's a symptom, not the disease?"

"Oh, he's a disease, too," Xarth said. "But not an original one. He's the political equivalent of foot fungus—always comes back, always looks worse than before, and no matter how much you try to get rid of it, some fool insists it's actually good for you."

Zog shuddered. He had no feet, but he understood the metaphor.

Xarth took another sip and stared at the swirling, iridescent liquid in his glass. "There was a time when Americans hated cults," he said. "Now they build them on purpose."

Zog raised a skeptical appendage. "Didn't they always have them?"

"Oh sure," Xarth said. "They used to call them religions, though, and at least those had the decency to involve invisible sky deities instead of bloated businessmen who can't spell 'hamburger.'"

Zog chuckled. "What changed?"

Xarth sighed. "People used to want leaders who inspired them. Now they want leaders who make them feel okay about being awful. You see, the great trick wasn't making people believe in him—the great trick was convincing them that if he was terrible, but still powerful, then maybe being terrible wasn't so bad."

Zog shook his head. "That's bleak."

"Oh, it gets worse," Xarth said. "You ever try arguing with someone in a cult?"

Zog thought for a moment. "I once tried to convince an Alurvian priest that his god wasn't actually the giant flaming gas cloud he worshiped but rather just a malfunctioning intergalactic sewage vent."

Xarth raised his glass. "And how'd that go?"

"He tried to set me on fire."

Xarth nodded. "Yeah. That's about how it goes down there, too."

Zog sighed and refilled both their glasses. "They'll never catch on."

Xarth chuckled, shaking his head. "Not as long as the hats keep selling."

CHAPTER 7: THE FREE SPEECH ZONE

Glorpnax adjusted the controls of the tender, guiding it toward what America's (Oops—'Merica) government had officially designated a "Free Speech Zone." The passengers peered out through the viewing panel, expecting something grand—perhaps an agora of passionate orators, a digital amphitheater of unrestricted discourse, or at least a well-maintained park bench. Instead, they found a fenced-off patch of land wedged between a sewage treatment plant and what appeared to be a decommissioned rollercoaster, its faded sign still promising "The Ride of Your Life!" The irony did not go unnoticed.

Spliv wrinkled his snout. "Why is their free speech confined to an area that smells like digestive failure?"

Grib, ever the realist, sighed. "Maybe, because if it were in a nice place, people might actually use it."

Glorpnax, who had once witnessed a civilization perish because they had decided fire was too unpredictable to be trusted, nodded sagely. "Limited speech in a limited space. Efficient."

In the center of the zone stood a lone Earthling, a middle-aged man sporting an unkempt beard, cargo shorts, and a tinfoil hat folded with the precision of a military engineer. He clutched a homemade sign that read, "HONK IF YOU'RE OPPRESSED BY MICROSCOPIC ALIENS."

"Oh good," Grib muttered. "A scholar."

The man, unaware of the presence of the invisible tender, however, immediately perked up. He waved frantically, then pointed to his sign with the enthusiasm of a man who had finally found an audience that might appreciate his work.

"Greetings, intergalactic travelers!" he bellowed. "I am Bartholomew Butterfield, the last sane man on this planet!"

Spliv squinted. "I find that highly unlikely. How does he know we are here?"

Glorpnax chuckled. "He doesn't. We're invisible remember? He just thinks we're here, like so much else he believes."

Bartholomew cupped his hands around his mouth and shouted. "I know you're there! You can't fool me! I can see through the lies, the deception, the government-issued fog that blinds the masses!"

Grib turned to Glorpnax. "He sees through fog? That's actually quite impressive."

"It's a metaphor," Glorpnax said. "And a bad one."

Bartholomew ran up to the fence that separated him from the rest of society, gripping the chain links as if he were a caged animal in an existentialist zoo exhibit. "You've come at last! I knew it! The Reptilian Overlords thought they could suppress the truth, but they couldn't suppress me!" He jabbed a finger at his temple. "I see what they don't want me to see!"

Glorpnax consulted his notes. "Reptilian Overlords? I don't see any mention of Reptilian Overlords.""

Bartholomew nodded violently, his tinfoil hat slipping slightly before he repositioned it. "They run everything. Government, media, the snack food industry— all of it! They communicate through microwaves! Have you ever wondered why every convenience store in America has a microwave? It's mind control, my friends. Mind control!"

Grib scribbled something in her notebook. "Microwaves? I thought humans used those for reheating questionable leftovers."

"Oh, they do," Glorpnax sighed. "But they also use them for secret mind control. Didn't you know? Wait for it."

Bartholomew leaned in as though revealing an ancient secret. "These microwaves... they make people complacent. They make them accept things like 'Free Speech Zones' and sixteen different brands of toothpaste that are all owned by the same company."

Glorpnax smiled, or at least it appeared similar to a smile. "Told you so."

The Trixlians exchanged glances.

"I mean," Spliv said, scratching his head, "he's not entirely wrong."

Bartholomew tapped his forehead knowingly. "They tell you it's just for cooking! That's what they want you to think. But if you adjust the frequency just right—" He wiggled his fingers mysteriously. "—you can implant thoughts into people's brains. That's why I wear this."

Bartholomew pointed to his foil hat that gleamed under the sun like some sort of homemade crown.

Mleeb sighed, exhaling loudly enough to rustle the weeds. "Another one of those humans. Why do they all think hats will save them?"

"Because it's cheap," Glorpnax said. "And humans love cheap solutions to complicated problems."

Spliv wrote: *Humans believe they are free thinkers. Most of them think the same thing: that someone else is secretly in charge.*

Bartholomew scoffed. "Sure, everyone thinks I'm crazy! But tell me this—if I were crazy, would I be able to quote the Federal Telecommunications Act of 1996 from memory?"

"I don't think those two things are mutually exclusive," Grib muttered.

Bartholomew continued, "And another thing! You ever notice how every time a major political scandal happens, they suddenly release a new flavor of snack chip?

It's a distraction! The Reptilians know that humans can't resist a limited-time nacho experience!"

Glorpnax jotted down a note: *Investigate Earth's snack-based social control policies.*

Meanwhile, a security drone hovered into view, blinking red in a way that suggested disapproval.

Grib blinked. "Birds?"

"Surveillance drones," Bartholomew repeated. "That's why pigeons never look you in the eye. They know."

Mleeb rubbed her temples. "I need a drink."

"I need several," Glorpnax muttered.

"Attention, Citizen Butterfield, "the drone's mechanized voice boomed. "You have exceeded your daily allotment of expressive enthusiasm. Please vacate the Free Speech Zone immediately."

Bartholomew paced back and forth, his paranoia reaching a crescendo. "They silence me! They put me in this so-called Free Speech Zone so no one will listen! They want you to think we have free speech, but it's all a trick! A dirty, rotten—"

Just then, a garbage truck rumbled by, drowning out the rest of his sentence. He threw his hands in the air as if to say, See? Proof!

Spliv tilted his head. "So, the humans created a designated space where one can say anything, but only in a location where no one will ever hear them?"

Glorpnax nodded. "That's how free speech works here."

Spliv wrote: *Humans value free speech. So much so that they store it in a secure, isolated facility, far away from actual society.*

Bartholomew turned his eyes skyward. "But you, oh wise beings from beyond, you understand, don't you? You know what's really going on! They'll come for you too, you know. They always do."

The Trixlians, in unison, took one step backward.

"Well," Glorpnax said, clearing his throat, "this has been educational, but I believe we should be on our way."

Bartholomew frantically tried to climb the fence. "Wait! Take me with you! I can be useful! I have a podcast!"

The Trixlian family hurried back to the tender as the drone emitted a sharp buzz and zapped Bartholomew's sign, reducing it to a smoldering pile of cardboard. As the tender lifted off, Bartholomew yelled after them, shaking his fists at the sky. "Don't trust the nacho chips! The cheese dust is full of lies!"

Inside the tender, Spliv watched as the Free Speech Zone grew smaller and smaller, eventually blending into the landscape of strip malls and highway overpasses.

"That was something," Grib muttered.

Glorpnax exhaled. "Indeed. But let us not be too quick to judge. Every species has its eccentrics."

Spliv leaned forward. "Yes, but are their eccentrics the only ones who see the truth?"

Glorpnax didn't answer. He simply activated the tender's drive sequence. But in the silence, the question lingered.

***

Xarth swirled his Cosmic Regret drink pensively, its toxic glow reflecting off his translucent skin. "You know, Zog," he said, his eyes blinking in asynchronous patterns, "I've been thinking about this whole 'free speech' thing the humans are so obsessed with."

Zog, polishing a glass with several of his appendages, raised what passed for an eyebrow. "Oh? And what profound insights has the Cosmic Regret bestowed upon you this time?"

Xarth exhaled, producing a noise reminiscent of a deflating balloon animal at a particularly depressing children's party. "It's all a joke, Zog. A cosmic prank played on a species too dense to get the punchline."

"How so?" Zog asked, sliding another glowing concoction towards a patron who looked like they'd seen better millennia.

"They've got these 'Free Speech Zones,' right? Little plots of land where they're allowed to say whatever they want. But they're always in the most godforsaken places. Next to sewage plants or abandoned amusement parks. It's like they're saying, 'Here's your freedom, but we've made it so unpleasant you won't want to use it.'"

Zog chuckled, a sound like gravel in a blender. "Efficient, though. Keeps the rabble-rousers out of sight, out of mind."

"That's just it," Xarth continued, gesticulating with his drink and nearly spilling it. "They think they're free because they can shout into the void. But the void doesn't shout back, Zog. It just swallows their words and burps out indifference."

A nearby patron, a gelatinous blob with too many eyes, hiccupped and oozed off its stool.

"You should've seen this human I observed on my last excursion," Xarth said, his voice dropping to a conspiratorial whisper. "Can't remember what he called himself. Ranting about about this and that . . . oh, and mind-control microwaves. And you know what? He was the only one there—in the 'Free Speech Zone.' Just him and his tinfoil hat."

Zog nodded sagely, or at least as sagely as an eight-armed bartender can nod. "Ah, the tinfoil hat. A classic Earth accessory. Pairs well with paranoia and a complete misunderstanding of how electromagnetic waves work."

"But here's the kicker, Zog," Xarth leaned in, nearly dunking one of his front eyes in his drink. "What if he's right? What if, in their backwards way, these conspiracy nuts are the only ones who see through the charade?"

Zog paused mid-polish. "That's a disturbing thought."

"Isn't it?" Xarth downed the rest of his drink in one gulp, shuddering as it burned its way down. The sensation was not unlike swallowing a small sun. "A species so convinced of its own freedom that it willingly confines its dissent to designated areas. Areas that smell like... well, let's just say it's the olfactory equivalent of humanity's hopes and dreams." He paused, his eyes fluttering a bit. "Rotten, decaying, and oddly reminiscent of yesterday's buffet special."

Zog refilled Xarth's glass without being asked. "Sounds like Earth alright. Always thinking they're at the center of some grand cosmic drama."

"And the saddest part?" Xarth continued, his voice tinged with something between pity and amusement. "They think they're unique. Special. The only ones struggling with these issues. Meanwhile, half the galaxy is watching them like some sort of reality show."

"Well," Zog said, his appendages gesturing expansively, "at least they provide good entertainment. And good business for bars like this one."

Xarth nodded, raising his glass in a mock toast. "To Earth then. May they never realize how absurd they truly are. It would ruin the show for the rest of us."

"To Earth," Zog agreed, clinking a glass against Xarth's with one of his many arms. "Where free speech is alive and well, as long as you don't mind shouting at sewage plants."

And so they drank, two cosmic beings finding humor in the follies of a species that thought it was alone in the universe. Meanwhile, somewhere on the blue marble below, Bartholomew Butterfield adjusted his tinfoil hat and prepared for another day of speaking freely to absolutely no one.

CHAPTER 8: THE TOURISTS WITNESS EARTH LOGIC IN ACTION

Glorpnax had guided thousands of intergalactic tourists across the universe, through nebulae shaped like cosmic jellyfish and planets where gravity was just a polite suggestion. He had explained the cultural rituals of the methane-breathing aristocrats of Zog-Tal Prime and the economic theories of the four-headed financiers of Vree-9. He had never, however, been asked to explain why a group of creatures with opposable thumbs and access to infinite knowledge chose to argue against it.

This, he knew, would be a challenge.

The tourists, packed into their cushy little tenders like larvae in a luxury cocoon, descended toward their next excursion with the quiet reverence of explorers approaching a sacred ruin—the school board meeting. Some adjusted their holographic notepads, eager to document the rituals of a species that had unlocked the secrets of the atom but still struggled with the concept of long division. As the tenders touched down, a hushed excitement spread among them—few had ever witnessed a deliberation on whether or not to teach children things they didn't already know.

The School Board Meeting was held in what Earthlings called a multi-purpose room, which meant it could be used for anything from education to indoor volleyball to pancake breakfasts honoring war veterans. It was decorated with faded posters reminding children that "Reading is FUNdamental!" and "Math is COOL," neither of which were statements the gathered adults seemed to agree with.

A long table sat at the front, behind which five people who did not want to be there sat in metal folding chairs. These were the School Board Members, a species of human that had no real power but absorbed a great deal of public anger, much like lightning rods installed to prevent a building from catching fire.

Opposite them sat the Parents, a larger and more diverse group, bound together only by their belief that their ignorance was just as valid as a doctorate. They arrived armed with highlighted printouts from dubious websites, anecdotes about a cousin's neighbor's son who "turned weird" after reading too many books, while others waved highlighted copies of books they had not actually read but had very strong feelings about. A few simply sat there, arms crossed, radiating the quiet fury of people who had once been told they were wrong and had never quite recovered. Their natural enemy, of course, was knowledge, which they viewed with the same suspicion one might reserve for a rattlesnake in a daycare center. And their battle cry was simple and majestic: "I pay taxes!"

"Observe, fellow travelers," Glorpnax began, gesturing at the collection of Earthlings who had gathered to reshape the minds of their offspring. "You are witnessing what is known as a 'debate.' This is a method humans use to determine truth, which often involves the loudest one winning."

Spliv squinted his large eyes. "I thought truth was based on evidence."

Glorpnax made a noise that sounded like a dial-up modem giving up. "That was the case for many centuries, but in the last few decades, truth has become more flexible."

A woman with a rigidly hair sprayed helmet of blonde hair took the microphone. She wore a T-shirt reading "WAKE UP SHEEPLE" and had an expression that suggested she had never once questioned a thought that entered her own head.

"Now, I'm just a simple mom," she began, though her social media activity suggested she spent 14 hours a day yelling at strangers. "But I don't want some fancy scientist tellin' my kids what's what! I read on Facebook that these so-called science books are teaching our children lies! Lies about evolution! Lies about climate change! Lies about outer space!" She paused dramatically. "Do we even know outer space is real? Has anyone here been?"

The room murmured in agreement. A large, burly man in a camo hat nodded solemnly.

Spliv's jaw fell open. "But . . . we're from outer space. We're here right now."

Mleeb patted his tiny shoulder. "Hush, dear. I think they're still warming up."

A man with a very large American flag on his shirt and a very small mustache on his face stood up next. "Now listen, folks. We all know that science is fine for some things. Like making gasoline and cell phones. But when it starts tellin' us things we don't wanna hear, well, that's just brainwashing! I say we teach our kids the old-fashioned way—through faith, common sense, and YouTube videos!"

The room erupted in applause.

Grib frowned. "Mother, am I misunderstanding something, or are these people fighting against knowledge itself?"

Gorvax nodded sagely. "You understand perfectly."

"But why?" Spliv asked. "Isn't that like fighting against air or gravity."

Glorpnax gave a knowing smile. "Ah, excellent observations! Earth logic is unique. Knowledge is suspicious because it sometimes makes people feel bad. When information arrives that contradicts a firmly held belief, the human brain experiences distress. Instead of adapting to new information, many Earthlings prefer to destroy the information altogether."

The meeting continued, now entering its most dramatic stage: the part where one particularly sweaty man stood up and yelled about "indoctrination" while not understanding the word in any meaningful way.

"I ain't lettin' my kid be brainwashed! The government is usin' these books to turn our children into sheep!" His voice cracked. "If my kid wants to learn science, he can do it the way God intended—by watchin' old episodes of MythBusters!"

The crowd cheered.

Mleeb leaned toward Glorpnax. "Tell me, dear guide, why do they fear knowledge so much?"

"Ah, a philosophical question! It is because knowledge requires change. And change is frightening. It is much easier to double down on an incorrect belief than to admit fault. On this planet, admitting you are wrong is seen as a personal failure, rather than a step toward wisdom."

Grib tapped her chin thoughtfully. "On Trixlia, when we're proven wrong, we celebrate, because it means we've gained a new truth."

Glorpnax nodded. "Yes, well, here, when a human is proven wrong, they become very loud and buy a bigger truck."

At that moment, a weary, overworked science teacher attempted to speak. Her glasses were askew, her expression one of pure despair. "I have a PhD in biology. I have spent years studying this subject. I can assure you that evolution is real, climate change is happening, and space is not a government conspiracy."

The room fell silent for a moment. Then someone shouted, "NERD!" and the crowd roared with laughter.

Spliv looked up at his father. "Do they think intelligence is bad?"

Gorvax nodded. "Yes, son. Here, intelligence is seen as an attack."

"What happens if you're too intelligent?"

Glorpnax sighed. "You move to another country, or you run for office and immediately lose."

The meeting ended with a unanimous decision to replace science textbooks with "Patriotic Earth Studies," a curriculum designed by a man who claimed to have met Jesus in a Walmart parking lot.

As the tourists left, Spliv held his father's hand tightly. "I feel sad, Father. Those children will never learn the truth."

"Yes, my son. But remember: the children who do learn the truth will one day grow up and write the rules."

"Unless the ones with the big trucks stop them first," Grib added.

Glorpnax clapped his appendages together. "A fantastic takeaway! Let's all give a round of applause to humanity, a species that once walked on the Moon and now questions if the Moon is real!"

The tourists returned to the tender, full of questions, concerns, and—above all else—a profound sense of relief that they were only visitors.

***

Xarth stared into his drink, a swirling purple abomination that could corrode titanium but was considered "mild" by his species. The bar, tucked into the dimmest, loneliest corner of the ship's entertainment wing, was nearly empty, save for the occasional patron nursing the consequences of existence. The ship hummed softly, gliding around the Earth as if it had somewhere better to be.

Zog polished several glasses with his many appendages. It was unclear whether this was for sanitation or simply for something to do. "So," he said, voice smooth as liquefied regret, "how do you think the excursion went?"

Xarth chuckled, though he didn't sound amused. "If it's like the last one I took, they went to a school board meeting."

Zog flinched as if someone had thrown a rock at his skull. "Ouch. That's rough."

"Yeah." Xarth took a sip, letting the drink remind him he was still alive. "They used to worship scientists. Used to put them on stamps, named entire institutions after them. Now they call them liars if they don't like what they hear."

Zog sighed, setting down the glass. "Well, the truth has never been as popular as a good story. Truth just kinda sits there, being all difficult. A good story, though—now that can make a man rich, electable, or the proud owner of a very large boat."

Xarth nodded, as if that explained everything. Maybe it did.

"They used to want to understand things," he said after a long pause. "Now it's just about winning arguments. Being louder than the other person. More obnoxious."

Zog wiped down the counter, even though it was already clean. "Hell of a thing."

Xarth leaned forward. "I remember one guy—big fella, red face, veins popping out like angry worms—he stood up and declared that 'theory' means 'guess.' Said it with the confidence of a man explaining water to a fish. I betcha they heard the same thing down there today. Very popular saying, you know."

Zog winced. "Oof. That's a tough one."

"You ever hear someone yell the phrase 'Gravity is just a theory' while standing firmly on the ground?"

Zog exhaled slowly. "Seriously. For flurp's sake. They ever wonder why they don't just float away?"

Xarth shrugged. "Apparently, it's just God holding them down."

Zog nodded like this was reasonable. "That's nice of Him or Her or Whomever."

"Thoughtful, really."

Xarth took another sip, let it burn a little. "Then there was this woman—had a binder labeled Real Facts. Brought it up to the microphone like it was the Rosetta Stone."

"Oh, good," Zog said. "Love a well-sourced argument."

"Pulled up a screenshot from a social media site called Patriot Mom Daily. Read it aloud like she was unveiling a sacred text. Declared that textbooks are 'full of government-approved propaganda' and 'numbers are suspicious.'"

Zog set down his rag, folded his appendages. "Gotta say, that's pretty impressive. Just throwing out numbers entirely. They must have a hell of a time at the grocery store."

Xarth nodded. "I imagine a lot of shouting at the check-out."

Zog whistled. "And what did the school board do?"

Xarth sighed. "Same thing they always do. Nodded solemnly, thanked everyone for their 'thoughtful concerns,' then promised to 'review the materials.'"

Zog poured another drink. "And what does that mean?"

"It means they're going to pretend to think about it for a while and then pray everyone forgets."

"That's Earth logic."

Xarth smirked. "It sure is."

They sat in silence for a while, the vastness of space stretching endlessly outside the window.

Zog slumped against the bar, massaging what might generously be called his forehead, if one were feeling charitable about alien anatomy. "You ever wonder how these Earth creatures managed to fling themselves at that moon of theirs?" he asked, his voice a mixture of awe and exasperation. "I mean, they can barely tie their own shoelaces without starting a war, but somehow they stuffed a few of their kind into a tin can and hurled it into space. Makes you wonder if the universe has a twisted sense of humor, doesn't it?"

Xarth exhaled. "Yeah. And I try not to."

Zog nodded, understanding completely. "Another drink?"

Xarth held up his empty glass. "Might as well. Logic's dead, but liquor's still kicking."

And they drank to that.

CHAPTER 9: THE FRIED-CHICKEN CONFLICT OF 21ST-CENTURY EARTH

The tour group materialized inside a fast-food establishment cleverly named "Chik-It-To-Me!", a name that surely had once been tested in focus groups full of tired and underpaid humans who were given coupons for their participation. The logo featured a chicken who was either screaming in terror or winking seductively. It was hard to say.

Spliv tugged on his father's elbow. "Are we inside a food temple?"

Gorvax observed the surroundings. Fluorescent lights buzzed overhead. A menu screen flickered, showing a poorly animated chicken giving a thumbs-up. The air smelled of grease and human desperation.

"Yes," Gorvax answered. "A food temple dedicated to the worship of the cheapest possible calories."

The tourists shuffled in, their cloaking devices ensuring that the human patrons remained blissfully unaware of the alien presence. A sign near the counter read:

OUR CHICKEN IS NEVER FROZEN!

(except when it is, which we are legally required to disclose in fine print.)

Grib whispered to her mother, Mleeb. "Why do the humans require a sign to tell them whether or not their food has been frozen?"

Mleeb furrowed her reptilian brow. "I assume it's because their senses have dulled to the point that they can no longer distinguish between fresh and frozen flesh."

"Ah," Grib said. "That makes sense."

"Evolution has been cruel to them," Mleeb added.

At that moment, a human conflict erupted near the counter.

"I told you," said a very large man in a red football jersey, veins popping in his forehead, "Chik-It-To-Me! has the greatest chicken sandwich in the world. It's called the Chik-a-Dee!"

"You absolute moron," sneered a lean man. "Everybody knows their Cluck-Daddy is their best sandwich."

The two men squared off. The air between them bristled with the kind of tension that, in other species, usually precedes an extinction event.

Spliv nudged his father. "They appear ready to engage in mortal combat."

"Over chicken," Mleeb added.

"Indeed," Gorvax confirmed. "This is what scholars refer to as 'a priority shift.'"

The football jersey man threw the first punch. The lean man ducked, narrowly avoiding catastrophe. But the impact sent a plastic tray flying across the room, where it landed on a child's head, sparking a secondary conflict.

A third combatant, a very large woman in yoga pants, jumped into the fray, shouting, "This whole conversation is pointless! Every true American knows that their best sandwich is the Bucky-Chik-a-Doodle!"

More humans joined in. A man wearing a T-shirt that said LIVE, LAUGH, LITIGATE attempted to restore order by filming the chaos with his electronic rectangle while shouting, "This is gonna go viral!"

Glorpnax sighed and addressed the tourists.

"This is a typical display of modern Earth diplomacy," he explained. "As you can see, differences of opinion often lead to ritualized combat."

Spliv's eyes widened. "So, they resolve their conflicts with war?"

"No," Glorpnax corrected. "That would require organization and clear objectives. This is something much stupider."

The tourists nodded, fascinated.

A human employee in a grease-stained uniform appeared from the kitchen, looking exhausted.

"Can y'all take this outside?" she mumbled, clearly paid too little to care whether or not people bludgeoned each other in the dining area.

Nobody listened to her.

Grib turned to her mother. "Mother, which chicken sandwich is actually the best?" she asked.

Mleeb thought carefully. "That is an excellent question, my dear. Let's examine the facts."

The Trixlian family observed the sandwiches being hurled across the restaurant as weapons. Some landed on the floor, untouched, their brioche buns glistening under the fluorescent lights.

After careful study, Mleeb concluded, "They're all identical."

Grib gasped. "Then why are they fighting?"

Gorvax answered grimly. "Because if humans ever stopped to think about how pointless their arguments were, their entire civilization would collapse overnight."

Spliv and Grib furiously took notes.

At last, the conflict began to wane. The lean man, bloodied but unbowed, grabbed a discarded sandwich off the floor and bit into it.

"Alright," he muttered. "Not bad."

The football jersey man, bruised and breathing heavily, picked up a rival sandwich and chewed thoughtfully. "Yeah. Yeah, this one's pretty good too."

The very large woman in yoga pants, a tear in her pants appearing, sat on the floor, exhausted. "Honestly, at the end of the day, it's all just fried bird meat."

The crowd slowly dispersed.

A moment later, a brand-new fight broke out at the soda fountain over whether Pepsi was better than Coke.

Glorpnax checked the local time—measured in arguments per minute—and gave a polite triple-blink to gather the tourists' attention. "That concludes today's cultural immersion," he announced in a series of polite clicking sounds. "Please return to the tenders. It's time to leave the humans of Earth alone with their slogans, their conspiracy theories, and their deep emotional attachment to corn syrup."

Some of the tourists sighed reluctantly, starting to catalog items they'd absconded with, souvenirs: a hall pass, a brochure for standardized testing, one of those electronic rectangles with an image of a monster truck on it. But most of the tourists were happy to leave Earth, because for some, it reminded them too much of their own planets before mandatory intelligence screenings were introduced.

They filed back into the tenders in orderly rows, still whispering in awe about the ritualistic power of chicken sandwiches and carbonated brand loyalty. Moments later, with a soft whir and a faint smell of ozone and regret, the vessels lifted skyward—whisked away to the comfort of the GLOMP-77, leaving Earth to do what it did best: misunderstand itself with remarkable enthusiasm.

***

Back on the luxury star cruiser, Xarth stared into his drink, a concoction that glowed with the intensity of a dying star and probably tasted just as apocalyptic.

Zog poured another round, his appendages moving in a choreographed dance of alcoholic efficiency. "What's got you down this time? Earth still giving you the cosmic blues?"

Xarth sighed. "They used to fight for freedom," he muttered. "Now they fight over stupid things. Like which bean juice is superior or whether their electronic rectangles should have buttons. God how they love their electronic rectangles."

Zog cleaned a glass with what might have been a tentacle or a very enthusiastic piece of kelp. "And?"

Xarth laughed bitterly, a noise that could curdle milk in a different galaxy. "And they don't even realize that the corporations selling them all these stupid things don't care which one they pick, so long as they pick something. It's like watching toddlers argue over which color crayon to eat."

Zog shrugged his many shoulders, a rippling motion that looked like a sentient wave doing the macarena. "Sounds efficient to me. Less thinking, more consuming. The American dream, right?"

Xarth nodded, his translucent skin shimmering with resignation. "Oh, it is. It's very efficient. That's the terrifying part. They've streamlined their own subjugation."

Zog wiped the counter and poured another drink, this one smoking ominously. "You know," he mused, his voice taking on the tone of someone who's about to say something profound or deeply stupid, "I saw a sign in a human news feed once. Said 'Jesus is coming.' What's that about? Some kind of traffic update?"

Xarth stared into his drink, watching the swirling colors that seemed to be having an existential crisis of their own. He thought about the sign. He'd seen several like it on past excursions. On highways. On barns. On billboards that also advertised all-you-can-eat buffets and discount colonoscopies.

"Jesus is always coming," Xarth muttered, his voice heavy with the weight of countless observations. "He's just never here yet. It's like promising an Earthling kid that Christmas is right around the corner, but the corner is on the other side of the universe."

Zog polished a glass with one of his lesser-used appendages, the one he usually saved for special occasions or particularly stubborn stains. "So, he's like a late bus? Or maybe a pizza delivery that got lost in a temporal loop?"

Xarth chuckled. "Something like that. Except the bus is invisible, the driver might not exist, and half the passengers are arguing about whether they're even on a bus at all."

"Sounds complicated," Zog said, his many eyes blinking in confusion. "Why don't they just, you know, look out the window?"

Xarth glanced at the spinning blue marble outside in the darkness of space. He sighed—the kind of sigh of someone who had once tried to explain credit scores to a jellyfish. "Because the window's plastered with ads for miracle diets, discount funerals, and limited-time-only happiness. The same people who sell the view also own the roads, the maps, and the illusion of choice. Hell, they probably trademarked the act of looking."

"You gonna keep staring at it?" Zog asked, flicking a tentacle like a bored teenager. "It's just a planet. One of trillions. Get over it."

Xarth took a slow sip of something mildly toxic and vaguely citrus, the kind of drink that made you question your life choices in a pleasant way. His gaze stayed fixed on the cloud-smothered globe below, watching the swirling clouds that hid a species too busy arguing to notice they were being observed.

"Yeah," he said, his voice a mixture of fascination and despair. "I think I will. It's like watching a perfectly built sandcastle get slowly swallowed by the tide. Inevitable, pointless, and strangely beautiful in its demise."

Zog nodded sagely, or as sagely as an eight-armed bartender can nod. "Well, as long as you're watching, might as well have another drink. This one's on the house. I call it The Death of Hope. Enjoy responsibly."

And so they sat, two cosmic beings, watching a planet spin below. Like a petri dish under a microscope. The inhabitants, of which, who were so convinced of their own importance, had no clue that they were being watched. Not by gods, not by demons, but by bored tourists looking for a cheap thrill, some easy laughs. Of course. What else would be happening?

CHAPTER 10: HOME AGAIN, HOME AGAIN, JIGGITY, JIG

Xarth downed The Death of Hope and watched Earth shrink into the distance. There it went—the little blue marble, rolling straight into the cosmic gutter. It had once been the perfect place for life, which naturally meant its inhabitants spent most of their time figuring out how to kill each other over imaginary lines and poisonous opinions. Now it was just another forgettable speck in the universe, a failed science experiment that had been left on the back of the stove until it caught fire. A miracle? Sure. But miracles, like lottery winnings, mostly ended up wasted on the worst people.

Zog slid another drink across the counter. "Humans . . . real committed to their own doom, aren't they?"

Xarth gave his glass a slow, contemplative swirl and let out a laugh—the kind that came with a receipt for disappointment. "Not all of them," he said. "But given the chance, most would livestream their own extinction. Probably with a sponsorship deal."

This got a chuckle out of Zog. "I kind of like those little critters—those humans. They're endlessly entertaining in the way a collapsing bridge is entertaining. The cables snapping, the slow-motion descent, the way they would stand there, electronic rectangles in hand, narrating their own demise."

The GLOMP-77 shuddered, like a giant metal beast with indigestion, as the tenders returned and docked. Most of them had gone down looking for something exotic— adventure, danger, meaning. Instead, they had found fast-food restaurants and souvenir shops. Humanity, it seemed, was less "boldly going" and more "boldly staying put."

A blob-like creature that might have been an alien or might have been a sentient bean bag chair oozed up to the bar, nearly engulfing Xarth. "Home again, home again, jiggety jig," it burbled, a kind of sigh.

"Jiggety jig?" Zog asked.

The blob-thing settled onto a stool that creaked in protest. It exhaled through what sounded like a kazoo being played underwater. "Human saying," it explained, waving what might have been an arm or might have been a particularly enthusiastic fold. "Picked it up from a biped who smelled like burnt sugar. Told me it's what humans say when they return to a place they never wanted to leave in the first place."

Zog wiped down the counter with an appendage that had, just moments ago, been scratching something it probably shouldn't have. "And what did you learn when you were down there?"

The blob shook what most likely was his head. "Terrible planet. Went on the excursion to see how they spend their leisure time. Nothing but advertisements and traffic. Everyone getting hustled by some guy in a costume."

"Which costume?" Xarth asked.

"Some sort of anthropomorphic rodent."

"Ah. Been on that one," Xarth muttered. "Seen that rodent."

"Humans had to pay just to stand in line," the blob continued, his gelatinous folds settling into place as he heaved himself onto a barstool. "Lines for food, lines for rides, lines to meet the rodent. And the food—my glorp, the food! Processed to the point of abstraction. They ordered something called a 'cheeseburger' and it arrived wrapped in five layers of plastic, looking like it had been printed instead of cooked."

Zog grunted and refilled Xarth's glass. "Sounds about right."

The blob shook his massive, wobbling head. "And the humans—by the stars, the humans! They all carried little screens, staring at them like they held the secrets of the universe. Every so often, one would pause to take a picture of their own face, looking miserable, and then go right back to staring at the screen again. I asked our tour guide what they were doing."

"Enlighten us," Xarth said, knocking back his drink.

"She told me they were 'making memories.'"

Zog let out a long, low whistle. "Damn shame. For most intelligent species you have to live through something to remember it."

The blob scoffed. "Not with this species! I guess they just collect pictures of themselves pretending to have fun, then go home and feel bad about it later." He took a long slurp from his drink, his multiple chins jiggling in protest. "And the worst part? They all knew it. Not a single one of them actually looked happy. Just tired. Like they had an obligation to enjoy themselves but weren't quite pulling it off."

Xarth sighed. "That's what happens when fun gets industrialized. You lose the beauty of the moment because you're taking too much time trying to capture it."

The blob-thing nodded. "Exactly. They paid for something called an 'experience package.' Thought it meant they were going to experience something. Turns out, it just meant they had permission to spend more money."

"Classic human move," Zog said, wiping down the bar. "Sell the illusion of happiness. Overcharge for the privilege."

The three of them sat in silence for a moment, contemplating the tragic absurdity of it all.

Then Zog clapped his hands, all eight of them at once. The sound was like a wet fish slapping against linoleum. "Anyway, next round's on the house. Because you're home now, and home is where you drink enough to forget where you just were."

The blob raised what might have been a glass, or possibly just a bubble trapped in its own protoplasm. "To home!" it gurgled.

Xarth raised his own. "To escaping with our wits somewhat intact."

He downed the glowing liquid in one gulp and signaled for another. Earth had that effect on sentient beings. It made them thirsty for forgetfulness, hungry for a reality that made sense.

Xarth turned back to the window. Earth was now barely visible. From here, it was easy to forget everything about it—the wars, the greed, the loud opinions shouted into the void. But down there, it all still mattered. They still had presidents and billionaires and reality TV stars, and they were still convinced they were the center of the universe.

"What about all the excursions you took?" Zog asked Xarth, squinting like he'd just remembered how to use his eyes.

"What about them?" Xarth replied, as if he were being asked about the consistency of mashed potatoes.

"I mean what did you learn on all those excursions?" Zog said. His voice had the sincerity of a malfunctioning diner bot trying to give back exact change.

Xarth blinked. He considered the question. Really chewed it. It was a good one. Not great. But good. And good questions were like asteroids with coupon codes—hard to find and usually ignored.

"I learned that humans don't actually want answers," Xarth said. "They just want better distractions."

Zog wiped the counter. "That's fair."

Xarth took a sip. "I also learned that they will pay an absurd amount of money for things they could do for free."

"Like what?"

"Like walking. Just putting one foot in front of the other."

Zog frowned. "Walking? You're pulling my appendages."

"Nope. They have these special rooms. Pay good money to walk in place. Call it a 'gym.' Even make it harder than regular walking. Because apparently, that makes sense."

Zog stared, all of his eyes blinking in disbelief. "You're making this up."

"Wish I was. Saw it myself. Right next to a shop selling pre-peeled oranges wrapped in plastic. Because peeling an orange is just too much work, I guess."

Zog shook his head. "No wonder they're circling the cosmic drain."

The gelatinous blob next to Xarth burped and chimed in, "Saw one human try to sell another one something called an 'NFT.'"

"Oh, yeah." Xarth smirked. "Those are a real hoot, to use an Earthling phrase."

"What do they do?" Zog asked, genuinely curious.

"They don't do anything," the blob replied.

"Then why do they buy them?"

"Because other people buy them."

Zog considered this. "Well, that's just plain stupid."

"Yes."

"And people are making money from it?"

"You betcha." The blob paused, then let out a gurgling laugh. "The more I think about it, the more I'm starting to like these humans."

"Of course you like humans," Xarth said, downing the last of his drink. "Everyone loves a good tragedy. It's like watching a star go supernova. Beautiful, in a catastrophic sort of way."

A rather polite chime rang out, signaling the ship was leaving Earth, like it did every Tuesday or so. Earth receded in the viewport, a blue marble spinning in the void, blissfully unaware of its audience.

"I almost feel bad for them," Zog said.

Xarth muttered. "Almost."

"They really think they're different from every other civilization that's burned itself out."

"They do," Xarth stared into his drink.

"They think they're going to be the first to get it right."

"They do."

The blob sighed, or at least it sounded like one. "But they won't, will they?"

"No," Xarth replied.

Somewhere deep within the GLOMP-77, the captain, an alien from a galaxy far, far away (which, for the record, isn't that far—about three or four light years, give or take, but who's counting?) rose from his command chair to address the passengers. He was a fine specimen, looking like the unholy lovechild of a basketball and a jello mold— if you've ever wondered what happens when entropy takes a vacation and leaves the universe to run its own terrible errands.

"Ladies, gentlemen, and sentient gas clouds," he began, his voice a rich blend of corporate smugness and cosmic indifference. "We are now leaving Earth and, by extension, its solar system. How was your stay on Earth? I trust you found it . . . memorable? If not, well, that's entirely on you, my dear travelers." He paused, giving his audience a chance to ponder their collective mistakes. "I hope you enjoyed the pyramids, or, for those of you who didn't, the traffic lights. We really try to give you the authentic human experience. Which, I should remind you, is a woeful, slow-motion car crash of a plan. But please, don't think about it too hard. If you do, you've got a lifetime of therapy ahead of you. Now, before we get to the fun part—hurtling into the cosmic void with absolutely no sense of meaning—let's go over a few safety tips for your return trip."

He cleared his throat, a sound that was both reassuring and vaguely suffocating. "First off, I don't expect we'll encounter any space pirates. But, if we do, we'll burst into hyperspace faster than you can say 'galactic loophole.' You won't feel it. Don't worry. We've got stabilizers that will keep the rolling to a minimum. It's really just a gentle tumble through the fabric of space-time. Also, several of you expressed concerns about diseases you may have picked up during your delightful excursions. Earth diseases—such a charming Earth tradition. Should you happen to catch something unpleasant, don't panic. We'll pass through a few cosmic dust clouds that will likely neutralize it. But do me a favor—don't touch anything sticky between here and Alpha Centauri. Trust me, it's for the best."

A nervous chuckle rippled through the ship, though it was unclear whether the passengers were more worried about space sickness or Earth-borne plagues. At this point, the distinction was mostly academic.

"Lastly," the captain continued, "I must inform you that we're gonna zip through some space junk and maybe a wormhole—don't worry about it. If things go wrong, just follow the flashing lights to your muster station where you'll be escorted to a far safer, more pleasant dimension. It's a bit of a lottery, really. Just think of it as a cosmic crapshoot. Enjoy the ride, folks. Have a wonderful evening aboard the grand GLOMP-77."

With that, the passengers, no longer quite sure whether they were on vacation or a very expensive form of cosmic therapy, shuffled toward the windows. They were eager to catch one last look at Earth before it disappeared behind them. They'd probably miss it, but not for the reasons they expected. Who could forget the endless debates about pineapple pizza, the beautifully dysfunctional government, the staggeringly unintelligent leadership, the charming disregard for civil liberties, the infectious diseases, the comforting hum of traffic jams, or the inexplicable, existential joy of reality television?

And then—poof—no more Earth. Like a rug yanked out from under a species. The GLOMP-77 zipped off into lightspeed with all the elegance of a drunk flamingo, abandoning humanity to whatever came next: barbecue or bliss, nobody could say. The passengers? Oblivious. Clueless. Slightly itchy. But hey, they had stories to tell, rashes to compare. Maybe even a pirate or two in their future. Wouldn't that be something?

Zog poured another round. "So, where to next?"

Xarth took his drink and grinned. "Someplace smarter, I hope."

Zog laughed. "Good luck with that."

CHAPTER 11: THE AFTERMATH OF OBSERVATION

Aboard the GLOMP-77, the passengers gathered in the ship's lounge. Most were dazed, exhausted, and somewhat sticky—though no one was willing to admit to what, exactly. The lounge was an admirable attempt at comfort, if one enjoyed the sensation of being trapped inside a vending machine from the year 1959. The chairs were soft, in a way that suggested they were judging you for sitting in them, and the lighting was dim enough to obscure any immediate regrets about the trip.

In the center of the room, Spliv and Grib, the two Trixlian children, sat cross-legged on the floor, their digital notepads overflowing with what might generously be called research notes, but what was, in reality, mostly crude sketches of humans doing inexplicable things.

Spliv pointed to his screen. "Look! This one human—he's staring at a small glowing rectangle and walking directly into traffic."

Grib scoffed. "That's nothing. I saw two of them arguing about whether water is wet. For three hours."

Glorpnax, the intergalactic excursion guide, cleared his throat (or, more accurately, emitted a sound reminiscent of a clogged drain). "Esteemed travelers, what have we learned?"

Phlubulox, a stick-like creature—maybe wood, maybe something else, something that looked like it had opinions—stood there, unimpressed. It didn't jiggle. It didn't need to. "That humans consider themselves intelligent, despite overwhelming evidence to the contrary."

A six-eyed amphibioid named Zarj raised a webbed hand. "That their economic system is designed to ensure that no one is ever satisfied, but everyone is constantly shopping."

Mleeb, ever the overprotective mother, sighed so loudly it registered on the ship's seismic sensors. "That their parenting strategies involve handing their offspring glowing rectangles filled with advertisements for products they don't need."

Glorpnax nodded approvingly. "Excellent observations. Now, let's summarize our key findings for the Intergalactic Bureau of Cultural Oddities." He pressed a button on his control pad, and a holographic report flickered to life.

Findings:

1. Humans are convinced they are the most intelligent species in the universe. They also eat food they know will make them sick and then complain about it.
2. They have created a system where they trade time for currency, then use the currency for things they don't have time to enjoy.
3. They believe they are free but must request permission to do almost anything fun.
4. Their offspring require constant entertainment, lest they begin forming their own thoughts, which is widely considered a disaster.

5. Humans have a device that can answer any question, yet they use it exclusively to argue with strangers and look at pictures of small, domesticated beasts.

6. Their government is run by the least competent among them, a system they call democracy, which ensures that only the most shameless rise to power.

7. The wealthiest among them control everything, but they are not called rulers. They are called "job creators," which seems to keep everyone pacified.

8. They have designed their society so that there must always be winners and losers, and they pretend this is fair, even though it clearly is not.

9. Their laws are so complex that even their own lawmakers don't understand them, but they pass more of them anyway.

10. They have institutions dedicated to teaching their young, yet most of their education comes from unverified videos made by strangers in basements.

Glorpnax sighed or at least made a noise that suggested cosmic despair, which, in his species, sounded a lot like a dishwasher giving up. "Well, at least they have snacks," he muttered, recalling the deep-fried concoction one human had lovingly referred to as a "corn dog." It had defied all known logic—why impale nourishment on a stick? Why batter it? Why deep fry it? Why, for the love of the cosmos, was it so delicious?

There was a chuckle from the crowd, followed by a moment of respectful silence for the absurd genius of human cuisine.

Spliv, still puzzled, tapped at his notepad. "But why don't they just fix their problems? They seem aware of them."

Rarvax, a veteran observer of primitive civilizations and part-time collector of novelty mugs (his favorite read 'I Went to Earth and All I Got Was This Existential Dread'), chuckled and smiled at Spliv. "Ah, my dear boy, because acknowledging a problem is far easier than solving it."

The crowd murmured in agreement. Xarth, who had finally dragged himself from the bar, leaned against the bulkhead, arms crossed. "They could fix things if they wanted to. But deep down, they enjoy the mess. Drama keeps them entertained. And entertainment is their true god. Ever seen one of their political debates? It's like watching two intoxicated squid wrestle over a traffic cone."

There was a collective shudder. Some of the passengers had, in fact, seen a human political debate. It had been screened on the ship as a horror-comedy double feature, right after The Shopping Channel.

Zog, appearing with a tray of drinks, raised an appendage. "Speaking of which, shall we toast to their inevitable implosion?"

The room erupted into laughter. Glasses (or the closest available equivalents) were raised, and for a moment, the great tragedy of humanity seemed almost poetic—if not entirely hilarious.

As the ship hummed onward, the passengers took comfort in one undeniable fact: at least they weren't human.

CHAPTER 12: ZOG'S THEORY OF EVERYTHING (AND OTHER HALF-BAKED IDEAS)

Zog wiped down the bar with an appendage that might have once been destined for something noble—perhaps delicate sculpture or interstellar diplomacy. Instead, it was now employed in the thankless task of smearing around a substance that smelled suspiciously like the aftermath of an Inglonian's questionable meal choices. (Inglonians, bless their eighteen stomachs, considered anything that used to scream a delicacy.) He sighed, which was quite the accomplishment for a being with no lungs, no diaphragm, and, if he was being honest, very little enthusiasm for the service industry.

Xarth sat hunched over his drink, which had the aroma of something that had second thoughts about existing. He gave it a swirl, watching it slosh against the sides of the glass like it, too, was trying to escape. Instead of contemplating the vast mysteries of the universe, he settled for the closest available equivalent: the bottom of his drink.

"You ever think about the meaning of it all?" Zog asked, plopping a fresh rag onto the counter like he was putting down a bet he already knew he'd lose.

Xarth exhaled through his nose slits. "Can't say that I have."

"Well, I have." Zog poured himself a shot of something potent enough to make lesser beings reconsider their commitment to having nervous systems. "And I think I've finally figured it out."

"Oh, this should be good." Xarth straightened up, suddenly intrigued. It wasn't every day a bartender unveiled a theory of existence between rounds of wiping up Inglonian mucus and pretending to listen to honeymooners.

"The universe," Zog said, gesturing with a tentacle that wobbled slightly, either from intoxication or the sheer effort of holding onto a thought, "is a giant, sentient garbage disposal."

Xarth blinked or was he simply passing gas. "Go on."

"All sentient life," Zog continued, "is just different forms of discarded food scraps. Some of us are moldy bread, some of us are week-old noodles stuck to the bottom of a takeout container, but at the end of the day, we're all just decaying matter, swirling around, waiting for the final grrrchhh"—he mimed the grinding noise of a disposal unit, complete with a shudder—"that sends us down the drain."

Xarth took a contemplative sip of his drink, considering the implications. If Zog was right, he was voluntarily consuming garbage, which, when he thought about it, wasn't much different from what humans did at convenience stores. He was too tired to be disgusted.

"Why a garbage disposal?" he asked. "Why not something more dignified? A great cosmic symphony? A celestial mosaic?"

Zog snorted. "I cleaned up after an Inglonian bachelor party last week. If that doesn't show you what the universe is really like, nothing will."

Xarth cringed. Inglonian bachelor parties were infamous for their destructive power, often classified as minor natural disasters on planets with a weak legal system.

"They puked in places I didn't even know existed," Zog continued, taking a solemn shot. "And as I scrubbed, I had a moment of clarity. The universe doesn't care about meaning. It doesn't care about destiny. It just chews things up, grinds them into smaller bits, and spits them out. And all the while, the scraps argue about which one of them is the tastiest."

Xarth rubbed his temples. "You're saying all conflict, all war, all philosophy—it's just old chicken bones and rotten lettuce debating their own importance?"

"Exactly!" Zog slammed his glass down with the kind of confidence only the deeply intoxicated possess. "The squid people of Zarnox think they're the chosen ones, the humans think they're the pinnacle of evolution, the Glorpans think they're the universe's greatest contribution to culture—when in reality, we're all just leftovers, waiting for the big cosmic disposal to flip the switch."

Xarth stared into his drink. "Depressing."

Zog shrugged. "I think it's liberating. You can stop trying so hard. Just accept that you're a half-eaten meatball rolling around the sink of infinity."

Xarth mulled it over. It was absurd, of course. Ludicrous. And yet—he had to admit, it explained a lot. Especially human behavior.

After a long silence, he raised his glass. "To being scraps."

Zog clinked his own against it. "To the drain."

They drank. The ship hummed softly, gliding through the void, carrying its cargo of leftovers toward whatever cosmic disposal awaited them.

There was a brief pause, the kind that settles in when two beings realize they may have just stumbled onto something far more accurate than they intended.

Then Zog poured another drink. "You know," he said, his tone shifting to the kind of voice a con artist uses before unveiling a scheme, "I've been thinking—what if we lean into this whole 'meaningless existence' thing? Market it?"

Xarth sighed. "I'm already regretting this."

"No, listen," Zog said, now on a roll. "People—well, creatures, at least—love meaningless stuff! That's why they pay for scented candles that smell like their dead ancestors or attend lectures about finding inner peace from guys who have clearly never felt peace a day in their lives. We take my theory, slap some marketing on it, and boom: we sell the Cosmic Garbage Disposal Philosophy as the next big thing in self-improvement."

Xarth stared at him. "You want to start a cult."

"Not a cult," Zog said, waving a tentacle dismissively. "A lifestyle brand. Huge difference. We'll sell overpriced merchandise. T-shirts that say 'I'm Just a Meatball in the Sink of Time.' Coffee mugs that say 'Drink Up Before the Drain Takes You.' A self-help book titled 'How to Stop Worrying and Accept That You're Trash.'"

Xarth sighed. "I hate that this might actually work."

"Of course it'll work! We'll get some washed-up celebrity from a doomed planet to endorse it. You know, someone with just enough name recognition to draw attention but not enough dignity to say no."

Xarth considered. "Yeah, Earth's crawling with that kind of person. A whole pile of losers to pick from. Especially the politicians."

"Perfect."

Zog leaned forward, excitement in his many eyes. "We'll need seminars, too. Make people pay exorbitant fees to hear the exact same nonsense they could've read in the book, but in a dimly lit room with overpriced snacks."

Xarth nodded. "We could sell 'purification retreats' in remote locations where we teach enlightenment through expensive deprivation."

"Yes! We take away their belongings, force them to subsist on nutrient paste, and at the end, they thank us for it."

"They pay us for it," Xarth corrected.

Zog grinned like a kid who'd just figured out how to make a paper airplane. "That's the spirit."

There was another long pause, punctuated only by the faint hum of the ship.

Then Xarth laughed, shaking his head like he couldn't believe his own thoughts. "So let me get this straight. We've gone from staring at the void to figuring out how to profit from it?"

Zog gave a thoughtful nod. "The universe may be pointless, but that doesn't mean we can't make money off it."

Xarth grinned. "You know, I'm starting to think there's a little human in you."

Zog burst out laughing. "Maybe we'll sell a few red hats that say, 'Make the Drain Great Again.'"

They clinked their glasses once more, this time not to mourn the absurdity of existence, but to squeeze a profit out of it. And somewhere, deep in the cold emptiness of space, the great cosmic disposal unit gave a low rumble, waiting for its next batch of leftovers.

CHAPTER 13: XARTH MAKES A DECISION

L ater in the evening, Xarth sat swirling a drink that smelled vaguely of burnt plastic and misguided optimism. The lights flickered halfheartedly, not for ambiance, but because the ship's electrical system had developed a personality disorder that nobody had the willpower to diagnose. Outside the viewport, Earth receded into the cosmic abyss, sparkling like a cheap bauble in a pawn shop window, advertising "Humanity - Slightly Used, As-Is Condition."

Zog wiped down the counter with an appendage that, biologically speaking, was meant for grasping small objects but had long since been repurposed for bar maintenance, back scratching, and the occasional unsolicited massage. "You coming back on the next cruise?"

Xarth exhaled through his nose slits, a sound that in his native language translated loosely to 'Absolutely not', and also, 'I regret all my life choices that led me here.' But he settled for a simple, "No."

For years, he had clung to a flicker of optimism, the way a doomed astronaut might cling to the last peanut in a vacuum-sealed snack pack—desperate, irrational, and ultimately meaningless. He had once believed that humans might stumble upon self-awareness, much like a sleep-deprived scientist stumbles upon a eureka moment—accidentally, with a lot of cursing, and usually after setting something on fire. But his last peek at Earth had snuffed that flame out quicker than you could say "nuclear winter." After listening to those who had recently visited Earth, the final nail in the coffin of his faith had been driven. Earth had become a black hole for optimism, sucking in any stray photons of hope and spitting out . . . well, nothing. Just the cold, hard vacuum of cosmic indifference. A real humdinger, that Earth. A real humdinger.

It wasn't the pollution, or the wars, or even the peculiar habit of exalting loud fools over quiet geniuses. No, what finally convinced him this species was doomed was a brawl he'd once witnessed—two grown adults, flushed and frothing, pummeling each other senseless over mayonnaise. Mayonnaise! Egg sludge! Xarth had seen species wipe themselves out over resources, over ideology, over mating rights. But condiments? Condiments were a new low. Even the most war-happy civilizations he'd studied at least had the decency to fight over something with a little more nutritional value.

"They have a saying on Earth," Xarth said.

"Oh, what's that?" Zog took the bait.

"Can't fix stupid," Xarth muttered, staring into his drink. "They're in love with their own doom."

Zog nodded sagely, despite having no real understanding of human self-destruction beyond what was required to pass the Intergalactic Tour Guide Certification Exam. He slid a bottle across the counter. "So, what now, my friend?"

Xarth caught it mid-slide, pocketed it, and gazed out at the stars. Somewhere out there, he thought, there had to be a civilization where intelligence wasn't treated like a contagious disease. A place where the smartest members weren't bullied into silence or ignored in favor of whichever loud idiot could string together the most words in the shortest amount of time.

"Somewhere out there," he said, standing up, "there's gotta be a planet where critical thinking isn't considered a personal attack."

Zog let out a low whistle. "Bold dream."

"Yeah," Xarth admitted. "But I figure the odds are still better than Earth figuring its shit out."

He made his way toward his stateroom, the ship humming softly around him. As he reached his stateroom door, GLOMP-77's intercom crackled to life. The ship had picked up an old Earth transmission, a message from decades past, still bouncing aimlessly through the cosmos.

A static-laced voice, full of naive optimism, rang out:

"We come in peace."

Xarth snorted. "Sure you do."

The ship jumped to hyperspace, leaving Earth and all its absurdity behind.

***

By the time Earth was just a smudge in the rearview mirror, most if not all the passengers of the GLOMP-77 were mentally and physically exhausted from what they saw. They sat in their staterooms muttering to themselves like war veterans who had seen things no one should see—things like daytime television and congressional hearings. All, that is, except young Vrilp who was not one to be deterred by logic, reason, or parental authority—three things he found increasingly inconvenient as he matured. As soon as his mother turned her many eyes away to lecture his older brother about the importance of "cultural respect," he did what any self-respecting young lifeform would do when denied something fundamentally ridiculous yet profoundly desirable.

He ever so quietly opened their stateroom door and snuck away.

He slithered, crept, and, at one point, tumbled dramatically toward THE COSMIC VENDING MACHINE OF THE GALACTIC LAUGHINGSTOCK, as if the universe itself were conspiring to slow him down.

But the universe, as always, had much bigger problems to deal with than one small alien trying to buy contraband dice.

Vrilp glanced around.

No one.

He reached into his pouch and produced his credits, which he had been saving for something important. Initially, he had planned to spend them on a limited-edition holographic card featuring Galactic Wrestling Champion Klarg the Unwieldy, but he had his sights set on something far more essential. Klarg would understand.

He inserted the credits and pressed the button labeled: "Alternative Facts Dice."

The vending machine whirred. It buzzed. It clanked in a way that suggested at least some of its parts were either sentient or deeply resentful of their job. The dice box slid forward, teetered on the edge of its slot, and—

Stopped.

Just stopped.

Sitting there.

Jammed.

Vrilp's gelatinous heart sank. He pressed the button again. Nothing. He pressed it a third time, because history had shown that when something did not work the first two times, the third time was often the charm. This was a lie, of course, but Vrilp was beginning to embrace the philosophy of his future dice.

He pounded on the glass. But the dice remained where they were, taunting him with their refusal to be acquired.

"Come on, you stupid Earth artifact!" he whined, his frustration bubbling over like a sun about to go supernova.

And that was when Tralg arrived.

She didn't say anything at first. She didn't have to. The sheer force of her maternal disappointment radiated through the air like an unspoken cosmic law.

"Vrilp," she said finally, in the kind of voice that suggested very bad things were about to happen to his freedom. "What are you doing?"

"Nothing!" he yelped, strategically placing himself in front of the machine as if he could physically conceal the evidence of his crime. "Just—uh—observing the mechanisms of an ancient human relic! Anthropological research!"

Tralg's many eyes narrowed. "Step aside."

"But—"

"Now."

Vrilp stepped aside.

Tralg stared at the vending machine, at the jammed dice, at the flashing sign that continued to insist reality was optional. She sighed the deep sigh of a mother who had too often witnessed the fundamental absurdity of the cosmos play out through her own offspring.

"Vrilp, I told you no."

"I just wanted to see if they worked!" he whined. "I wanted to roll a six every time! I wanted—"

"To live in a world where truth is whatever you want it to be?" Tralg finished for him. "Is that really what you want?"

Vrilp hesitated. "It sounds nice when you say it like that."

"It always does," she muttered. "That's the problem. Come on. We're leaving."

"But my credits!"

"Consider them a donation to the museum of poor decision-making. Oh, and you're grounded."

"What's that," Vrilp asked.

"It's something humans do," his mother sighed. "A quaint, almost medieval concept. You'll stay in the domicile unit until I tell you otherwise. You'll think about why you disobeyed me. And you';l contemplate the inherent epistemological instability of so-called 'Alternative Facts Dice.' Vrilp, did you truly believe that a random tumble of polyhedrons could generate verifiable truths? Those humans and their capacity for self-deception, neatly packaged in a vending machine – it's terrifying, really. Like selling bottled smog. They're doomed, of course, even with their remarkable ingenuity in the realm of nonsense."

As Tralg dragged her sulking son back toward their stateroom, Vrilp shot one last, longing glance at the dice, which remained trapped in the machine, forever on the cusp of being won but never quite attainable. His dreams of consequence-free reality faded with each step. A fitting tribute to the human condition. Or maybe just to human stupidity. Usually both.

Meanwhile, light-years distant, that little blue marble of delusion, Earth spun on, blissfully unaware that its greatest cultural export had become a trinket in a malfunctioning vending machine on an intergalactic cruise ship.

And maybe—just maybe—that was the punchline to the whole damn joke.

AUTHOR'S FINAL NOTE

Okay, so here we are at the end of this . . . this literary contraption. Like a carnival ride that's been deemed structurally unsound, but they let you ride it anyway, just this once. And you're probably expecting me to wrap things up neatly, tie up all the loose ends, offer some kind of profound, earth-shattering summation. But if you've made it this far, you know that's not really my style. Truth be told, I'm not even sure what I'm supposed to say at this point. "Thanks for reading?" Seems a bit trite. "I hope you enjoyed it?" Presumptuous, at best.

I guess what I'm trying to say is . . . well, I'm not sure what I'm trying to say. This whole process has been like trying to herd cats made of smoke. You think you've got a handle on things, and then poof! They vanish into thin air, leaving you with nothing but singed whiskers and a lingering smell of burnt ambition. I started out with the noble intention of skewering humanity's foibles, holding a mirror up to our collective madness, and making a few jokes along the way. But somewhere along the line, the mirror cracked, the jokes fell flat, and I found myself staring into the abyss, only to discover that the abyss was staring back, and it had a rather unsettling fondness for reality television.

And that's the thing about humanity, isn't it? We're a walking, talking, self-contradictory paradox. We're capable of extraordinary acts of kindness and breathtaking feats of cruelty. We can build soaring cathedrals and devastating weapons of mass destruction. We can write beautiful poetry and compose catchy jingles for erectile dysfunction medication. We're a mess. A glorious, spectacular, utterly baffling mess.

So, what's the takeaway here? What profound wisdom can I impart before I shuffle off into the literary sunset? Well, I'm not too sure. But I suppose it's this: don't take things too seriously. Laugh at the absurdity of it all. Embrace the chaos. And for God's sake, don't trust anyone who claims to have all the answers. Because the truth is, nobody knows what's going on. We're all just making it up as we go along, stumbling through the darkness, hoping we don't trip over anything too important.

And as for the real aliens who secretly visit us, well, maybe they'll learn something from their Earthly excursions. Maybe they'll come to the conclusion that Earth is the kind of place where lessons are hard to learn—if you don't mind making a mess while you try. Maybe they'll even get something useful out of it. Or not. Who knows? It's not like we have much to offer in the way of wisdom, but we do have a good collection of oddities. Or maybe they'll just write us off as a lost cause and move on to the next planet on their intergalactic itinerary. I suppose it doesn't really matter, does it now?

So, this is it. Farewell, my friends. May you laugh just enough to keep from screaming, may your nights be mercifully short on cosmic horror, and may you never, under any circumstances, find yourself trapped on a cruise ship with a Trixlian family, a bartender who looks like an anatomical prank, and a bitter extraterrestrial who drinks like the universe personally let him down. Afterall, life's a funny thing when you think about it.

ABOUT THE AUTHOR

Philip **Mazza** is a novelist with a boundless imagination, captivating readers with the epic fantasy series *The Harrow Saga*. Born in New York in 1959, he earned a degree in Business from LeMoyne College and an MBA, later holding leadership roles in human resources and operations. Now a professor at the Madden School of Business and Economics, Philip dedicates his time to his students and writing. *The Cosmic Vending Machine of the Galactic Laughingstock* is his eleventh literary work. He and his wife enjoy travel and continue to live in upstate New York.

www.ingramcontent.com/pod-product-compliance
Lightning Source LLC
Chambersburg PA
CBHW030330020726
47493CB00004B/1224